MANDY MORTON began her professional life as a musician. More recently, she has worked as a freelance arts journalist for national and local radio. She currently presents the radio arts magazine *The Eclectic Light Show* and lives with her partner, who is also a crime writer, in Cambridge and Cornwall, where there is always a place for an ageing long-haired tabby cat.

@icloudmandy
@hettiebagshot
HettieBagshotMysteries

05128619

By Mandy Morton

The No. 2 Feline Detective Agency
Cat Among the Pumpkins
The Death of Downton Tabby
The Ghost of Christmas Paws

a&b

The Death of Downton Tabby

MANDY MORTON

Allison & Busby Limited
12 Fitzroy Mews
London W1T 6DW
allisonandbusby.com

First published in Great Britain by Allison & Busby in 2016.

Copyright © 2016 by MANDY MORTON

A CIP catalogue record for this book is available from
the British Library.

First Edition

ISBN 978-0-7490-2060-6

Typeset in 11.5/16.6 pt Sabon by
Allison & Busby Ltd.

The paper used for this Allison & Busby publication
has been produced from trees that have been legally sourced
from well-managed and credibly certified forests.

Printed and bound by
CPI Group (UK) Ltd, Croydon, CR0 4YY

In memory of Polly Hodge and Mr Pushkin

CHAPTER ONE

Betty and Beryl Butter's bread ovens were going into overdrive as the day of the town's first literary festival finally arrived. There had been months of careful preparation, and most of the more outgoing residents had involved themselves at every level: as queens of pies, pastries and cakes, the Butter sisters had stepped forward to supply the throng of authors with the expected hospitality. As they retrieved the first batch of festival doughnuts from the fryer – ready for Beryl to roll in sugar – a legion of wordsmiths was already headed for the town to proclaim the merits of their latest novels to festivalgoers, all keen to dissect every word and leave happily with a personally dedicated copy of their favourite author's latest tome.

Hettie Bagshot and her sidekick Tilly Jenkins, who ran the No. 2 Feline Detective Agency from the back room of the Butters' high street bakery, had naturally been involved from the start. Hettie, for her sins, was appointed head of festival security, while Tilly had been able to indulge her passion for crime fiction by being entrusted with the booking of authors, poets and a sprinkling of what she liked to call 'musical interludes'. There had been a few hiccups along the way. The biggest howler arrived in the shape of the official festival poster, announcing the town's first 'Littertray Festival'. The mistake was unfortunate but not untypical of Dorcas Ink, the local printer, who was more than slightly deaf and had misunderstood the instructions given to her over the phone by Turner Page, Festival Director. With limited funds and a tight schedule, Turner had chosen to apply a blind eye to the mistake, taking heart instead from the list of correctly spelt authors' names on the lurid orange background.

Tilly had done a fine job, pulling together an exceptional line-up which included the cream of feline novelists and celebrities. The biggest scoop was to bag the aristocat-turned-author, Downton Tabby, whose books chronicling the lives of the upper crust and the lower orders had hit the TV screens in a big way and taken the country by storm. The Brontës of Teethly had also accepted Tilly's invitation, and all three sisters – known for their bonnet novels set against the backdrop of the Porkshire Moors – were to appear. The field of crime fiction was led by P. D. Hodge, known to her fans as Polly, who was conveniently local, owning a rather fine town house on the seafront at Southwool, where she summered each year. Appreciated for her generosity as well as for her talent, Polly Hodge was one of the main festival sponsors, which was probably why her name was so much bigger on the poster than anyone else's – although Dorcas Ink had been known to get her font sizes mixed up on more than one occasion.

Hettie decided to reserve judgement on the wisdom of holding a book festival in the town. When Turner Page was unseated from his job as chief librarian, and the library demolished shortly afterwards, Hettie and Tilly had both mourned the resource, if only for the loss of warm radiators on cold days. Then came Turner's mobile library, followed by the purchase of Furcross House; these days, Furcross was a flourishing library centre with space for community groups and activities, as well as a rather idyllic burial plot and memorial gardens dedicated to the late Marcia Woolcoat, one of the town's prominent philanthropists who had come to a sticky end during a case in which Hettie had been involved up to her elegant tabby neck.

Unlike Tilly, Hettie found socialising a bit of a strain, despite having lived much of her life on the front row. Her ability to reinvent herself when the going got tough was a quality to be admired, even though some of the turns in her road map were a little extreme. She had enjoyed a fairly successful music career back in the mists of time, and had tried being self-sufficient in a shed on the town's allotments until the great storm put paid to her shelter; more recently, due to a couple of high-profile cases, she and Tilly had pooled their limited resources and continued to run a seemingly professional detective agency. They were much in demand and revered by most of the community for their knack of getting to the bottom of things, but the downside of all this for Hettie was that she never seemed to have any time for herself; as she was by far the most interesting cat she knew, socialising was always a bit of a let-down. Tilly, of course, was the exception, and probably the best thing that had ever happened to Hettie; inviting her to share the back room at the Butters' bakery still ranked as one of the best ideas she'd ever had. The two cats propped each other up through thick and thin, and Tilly was rare in her ability to handle Hettie's moods and outspoken views with the patience and humour they deserved.

Tilly had hardly slept. The summer heatwave had been relentless and all but unbearable for long-haired cats, and now that the bread ovens were underway in the corridor outside their room, she knew that any further attempt at sleep was futile. She scrambled from her cushion and stretched her arthritic limbs; the pain was nowhere near as bad in the summer, but she still had to coax her swollen joints into life. Hettie was out for the count in her armchair, lying on her back in a twisted, somewhat ungainly fashion, with legs sprawled in every direction and a mass of long, peach-coloured fur exposed to the elements.

Tilly padded to the kettle and prepared two mugs for their morning tea. She opened the curtains to reveal the first rays of a sun that had hardly gone down before offering the promise of another scorching day. Looking out on to the backyard, she marvelled at the striking reds of the potted geraniums, contrasting with the deep blue lobelia. It was her favourite time of year, when everything was still new and vibrant and before the stress of high summer exhausted the colours.

'Shut the light out! It can't be time yet,' came a bad-tempered voice from behind her. Tilly turned to see the crumpled heap in the armchair gradually gain some composure as Hettie Bagshot sat up. 'What time do you call this? It's the middle of the night. Don't think that by putting the kettle on you can pretend it's morning.'

Tilly giggled and poured hot water into the mugs as Hettie continued with her early morning observations. 'I can't believe that we've signed up to this festival for the whole bloody weekend. It's been months in the planning, and all it's doing is encouraging the stuck-up cats in the town to parade around with books under their arms, getting together for their nasty little reading groups where they just sit and gossip about other nasty little reading groups. And now we're about to be descended on by a bunch of authors planning to bore the fur off us with the intricacies of how they approach their work, the terror of writer's block, and whether they prefer pencils to typewriters.'

'You'll enjoy the music,' said Tilly, trying to put a more positive spin on Hettie's rant. 'Muddy Fryer is going to perform her complete Arthurian cycle for the first time ever.'

'Only because no one else would let her,' retorted Hettie, accepting her morning tea with very little grace. 'I can't understand why we're not having a proper festival with proper stages and proper music instead of all these books everywhere. Too many blurred edges if you ask me.'

Tilly could have pointed out here that no one *had* asked Hettie, but being confrontational before her friend had drunk her first cup of tea wasn't a good idea and could easily have ruined the rest of their day.

CHAPTER TWO

The clock on the staff sideboard said seven o'clock, much to Hettie's annoyance. Even in summer she never rose before nine, but on day one of the 'Littertray Festival' she had to concede that there was still a lot that needed to be done before they set out for Furcross House.

She threw on an old T-shirt, splashed some cold water across her face and positioned herself at her desk to try and make sense of the list of authors' names that Tilly had attempted to type out earlier in the week. As head of security, Hettie had insisted that all participants in the festival should wear lanyards with name tags; it hadn't occurred to her that she would be making them up herself and, as with most things Hettie took on, the last minute seemed exactly the right time to get on with the job.

Giving the list a cursory glance, she knew that she'd have to wait for Tilly to return from the breakfast queue in the Butters' shop: in the months they had been running their detective agency, Tilly's relationship with the typewriter had not improved and the list needed translating.

'Sorry I was so long,' said her friend, falling over the threshold with two large bacon baps. 'They've gone mad out there, all queuing down the high street for Betty's festival hampers. I think she wishes she'd never come up with the idea. Beryl looks a bit rattled, too, and the heat doesn't help. It's really warm out there already.'

Hettie pushed the box of lanyards to one side to make way for the breakfast as Tilly filled the kettle. 'What's she putting in the hampers? If they're that popular, maybe we should have ordered one. We'll need to take some food – I think it's going to be a long weekend, and it's only Friday.'

'No need – we're all found for two days once we get to Furcross. There's a hospitality tent in the memorial gardens for festival staff and authors – non-stop dinners, teas and suppers, and an all-day festival breakfast which finishes at two.'

Hettie was visibly cheered by Tilly's inside information on the comestible prospects for the weekend, although she was a little confused about an all-day breakfast which wasn't quite what it said on the frying pan. She took a sizeable bite out of her bacon bap, allowing the butter to linger on her chin. Tilly made the tea and joined her at the desk, where – for the next few minutes – all conversation consisted of appreciative grunts, followed by a round of satisfied licking and cleaning.

'I suppose I'd better get on with these name tags,' said Hettie, downing her tea in one go. 'I've been trying to read your list of names, but there seem to be more numbers than letters, which doesn't give me much to go on.'

Tilly stared down at her abortive attempt and had to agree that it did need more work, although she was convinced that the staff typewriter had had it in for her right from the start. 'I'll call the names out while you write them on the tags,' she offered.

'OK, but you'll have to spell them – some of these authors have such stuck-up names. Let's start with the Brontës as there are three of them. What are their first names?'

'Charlene, Emmeline and Ann,' said Tilly, tipping the lanyards out of the box and beginning to sort the red ones from the blue.

Hettie treated herself to a snigger and wrote out three name tags, passing them to Tilly for clipping on to the blue ribbons. 'You've got to put the dots over the "e",' Tilly said, passing them back. 'It's not proper without the dots.'

'What do you mean? What dots?'

'The dots over the "e" in Brontë. I think they call it an umalot or something.'

'"An umalot"? Whatever next? Shall I stick dots over all the "e"s to make them feel even more special than they think they are already?'

Tilly ignored Hettie's comment and reached for the staff dictionary. 'Here it is. "Umlaut: indicating the modification in the quality of the vowel".'

'Sod that,' grumbled Hettie. 'With all these bloody name tags to write, the quality is going to be poor across the board. Who's next?'

'Downton Tabby. I think he's titled but I'm not sure. He doesn't use it on his books, so plain old Downton will do.'

Hettie wrote out the name and passed the tag to Tilly. 'He's going to be my main problem this weekend. Everyone you speak to wants to meet him. High profile doesn't even begin to describe him. His publicist has asked for a private parking area for his Rolls-Royce and an escort at all times as he moves around the festival. I've asked Bugs Anderton to look after him – she's more than used to dealing with enlarged egos as she's got one herself.'

Tilly had to agree that the town's Friendship Club President was the perfect choice, but the clock on the staff sideboard had moved its hands to eight o'clock and only four name tags had been completed; with the festival's official opening at midday, there was still a long way to go.

Two hours later, all the festival authors and their entourages were threaded and ready to go, although Hettie's copperplate letters had descended into an erratic scribble with a few unwanted umlauts thrown in for good measure. Next came the red lanyards, bestowing an air of importance on those from the town who had stepped forward to help – or, more especially, to qualify for a free ticket.

'At least we know this lot,' sighed Hettie, taking up a new felt-tip pen. 'Reel them off.'

It was an impressive line-up; a battalion of the town's great and good: Delirium Treemints on refreshments; Lavender Stamp, postmistress, on tickets and passes; Irene Peggledrip and her spirit guide Crimola on the information desk and lost kittens; Poppa Phene, the plumber, on car parking and chemical toilets. The list stretched ever on, finishing with the vendors, those folk in the town who had taken advantage of the influx of visiting cats to boost their businesses: Elsie Haddock had invested in a mobile fish and chip van in direct competition to Greasy Tom's fast-food outlet; Tilly's best friend Jessie, who kept the charity shop in Cheapcuts Lane, was bringing her stall of cloche hats and rainbow knits; Meridian Hambone, who ran the high street's hardware store, had ordered boxes of hurriedly printed festival T-shirts and tote bags from Dorcas Ink, all boasting the word 'Littertray' in their branding; and Betty and Beryl Butter, being shrewd and businesslike, had won the jewel in the crown and had their images emblazoned all over the paper bags which would carry off the books and food bought at the festival.

'Just us to go then,' said Tilly, putting the red name tags in a box. 'You, me and Bruiser.'

Perfectly on cue, Bruiser Venutius popped his grizzly grey head round the door. 'Wotcha! 'Ow's it all goin'?'

Bruiser had been a friend of Hettie's for years. He was one of life's wanderers, never staying too long anywhere and thriving on his own company. He'd turned up one cold, frosty morning and had instantly been welcomed and adopted by the Butters as their 'lad about the yard', as well as being taken on by Hettie as driver of the No. 2 Feline Detective Agency's mode of transport, a fine bright red motorbike and sidecar which Tilly had christened Miss Scarlet. Bruiser and Miss Scarlet shared a purpose-built shed at the bottom of the Butters' garden, and due to his advancing years and the joy of a place of his own, his wanderlust had dwindled. Like Hettie and Tilly, he had become very much part of the Butters' family of displaced, but now settled friends.

'You're up early,' said Hettie, stuffing the final batch of lanyards into the box. 'Just in time to receive your official name tag. Here – stick that round your neck.'

Bruiser received his lanyard with pride and pulled it over his head as if he'd been given a gold medal. 'I s'pose Miss Scarlet will need one of them on-site parkin' things? Are you doin' them?'

'Mercifully that's Poppa's department. He's on parking and toilets.'

'Ah, I've seen 'im already today. 'E's up there now, markin' out the bays on the old cricket ground. 'E says we're expectin' 'undreds of cats from outside the town on account of Downton Tabby comin'.'

Hettie nodded sagely at Bruiser's words. 'Yes, I can see that he's a big attraction but he has the potential to be a bloody nuisance for the rest of us – and he's down to appear tonight *and* tomorrow, so we're stuck with him for both days.'

'But it's all very exciting,' said Tilly, lapsing into a surprisingly tuneful rendition of the theme to Downton Tabby's TV series, *In the Kitchens and Up the Stairs*.

Hettie groaned, as she did every week when the show was aired. She didn't mind the programme itself, but the aftermath of Tilly humming the tune constantly for days put her teeth on edge. 'I think we should make a move. I'll need to check entrances and exits before the hordes arrive and we've got to give out the name tags to the helpers. Are you free to run us to Furcross House, Bruiser?'

'Yep. I'm waitin' for another batch of stuff to run up there from the Butters, but they're so busy in the shop that they've given me a bit of a break, so now would be a good time.'

Bruiser left Hettie and Tilly to gather themselves together. The big question on a hot day was what to wear, and they needed to be smart but not too done-up. Hettie always relied on Tilly to strike the right note regarding fashion, but heatwaves were a real problem for any cat with long hair.

'I think I'm going *tabby chic*,' Tilly said, hauling a pile of clothes out from the bottom drawer of the filing cabinet and sorting through them.

'And what, dare I ask, is that?' Hettie was already getting irritated at the thought of having to discard the baggy T-shirt she was wearing, which was cool and comfortable.

'*Tabby chic* is posh scruffy,' explained Tilly as she burrowed through her extensive mountain of cardigans, rejecting all of them as too warm for the weather. 'We need to look like we haven't bothered but we have really, if you see what I mean.'

Hettie didn't see what Tilly meant at all and was beginning to think that the T-shirt she was wearing would do when a muffled cry of success came from the bundle of clothes. Tilly emerged triumphant. 'Look what I've found! I bought these at the Felixtoe Book Festival when I was scouting for authors – booky T-shirts! This one should fit you – it says *Lord of the Pies* on it. That's a lovely book about kittens being stranded on a desert island.'

Hettie didn't much care what the book was about, although she would happily subscribe to all kittens being stranded on a desert island, but the bright red T-shirt did look good and the title was a suitable comment to wear across her chest. She pulled it on, and had to agree that it was indeed *tabby chic*. Tilly had laid out three possibilities for herself, all bearing titles by one of her favourite crime writers. Nicolette Upstart was almost as prolific with her merchandise as she was with her novels, and Tilly had got overexcited when Nicolette's agent confirmed that she would come to the town's festival as long as she could bring her 'pop-up merch tent' with her. 'Which one shall I wear? They're all lovely.'

'What have you got to choose from?' asked Hettie, trying to look interested.

'*Two for Sparrows*, *Fur in the Sunlight* or *The Death of Lucy Cat*.'

'I think you should wear the yellow so you can stand out in a crowd. If you're looking after the authors, they need to be able to see where you are.'

'Good idea,' said Tilly. '*Fur in the Sunlight* it is, then.'

She returned the mountain of clothes to the filing cabinet, gave their mugs a quick rinse and picked up the box of red lanyards. Hettie jammed her sunglasses on her head, grabbed the box of blue lanyards and strode to the door just as the telephone began to ring in the staff sideboard.

The staff sideboard was the central hub of Hettie and Tilly's life. Its capacity for storing and, in some cases, hiding the trappings of life was boundless. Operating out of such a small room offered its difficulties, although Tilly had a knack for transforming the office into a comfortable bedsit on a daily and sometimes hourly basis. The staff sideboard was her rock: she kept everything in it and was the only one of the two cats capable of laying her paws on what they needed instantly from its limitless storage. The friends had both agreed that a telephone would be a good business asset but Hettie found it a gross intrusion on her psyche, which was why it lived out of sight and muffled by cushions.

Tilly abandoned her box and scrambled into the sideboard, while Hettie stood at the door waiting for news. 'Hello? The No. 2 Feline Detective Agency, Tilly speaking. How can I . . . I'm sorry, can you speak up? Who is this? I'm afraid you're a bit wispy. Oh, now you're cutting out altogether.' Tilly backed out of the sideboard, still holding the receiver in the hope that the reception would improve. 'Now, shall we start again? Who is this? Turnip, was that? Throat? Oh, I see – you have a sore throat, Mr Turnip.'

Hettie decided to intervene, realising that they would never get to Furcross House if Tilly continued to indulge Mr Turnip. She took hold of the phone. 'Hettie Bagshot speaking. How can I help, Mr Turnip? Oh, I see! Turner, not Turnip, Turner as in Turner Page. Whatever has happened to your voice? We're just on our way up to the festival now – do you need us to bring lozenges? You need me to what?! Interview Downton Tabby tonight? In front of all those cats? I couldn't possibly! I know nothing about him except for the TV show. You want me to be probing as if I'm on one of my cases? Can't you get someone else? Maybe if you suck a lozenge you'll get your voice back so you can do it as planned. Hello? Are you still there? I don't believe it! He's gone and landed me with the worst job of the whole bloody weekend.' Hettie slammed the phone back on the receiver and pushed it back into the staff sideboard. 'Well, that's put a real damper on the day. I knew Downton Tabby was a bad idea as soon as you'd booked him.'

Tilly giggled. 'Well, he sold the festival out in two days, and Turner Page is paying us well for all we're doing. It's a lovely job really – no violence or murders to solve, just two peaceful days in the sunshine.'

'I wouldn't be too sure about the murders,' said Hettie, picking up the box of blue name tags. 'I can think of one or two necks I'd like to wring, starting with yours!'

Hettie and Tilly emerged into a stiflingly hot high street to find Bruiser waiting with Miss Scarlet. Tilly clambered into the sidecar and Hettie was about to follow when a whirlwind blew out of the post office in the shape of Lavender Stamp, looking hot and bothered in a loud flower-print dress. Lavender Stamp was renowned for her offhand nature, and relished the spite she could administer along with stamps and postal orders at her counter. A trip to her post office was a trial to most of the town's residents, and she had always harboured a special animosity towards Hettie.

'Miss Bagshot! Wait! Are you going to Furcross House?'

Hettie was tempted to leap into the sidecar and ignore the oncoming floral print but Lavender was upon her before she had the chance. 'I wonder if I could commandeer your vehicle? I'm running late and I need to be at the festival ticket office as soon as possible.'

It was satisfying to dispense a favour to Lavender Stamp and Hettie rose to it, putting on her widest smile as the sarcasm spilt out onto the hot pavement. 'Why, Miss Stamp, it would be our greatest pleasure to offer you a lift. Have you ridden pillion before?'

Lavender stared at the motorbike through her

winged spectacles as Bruiser kicked the engine into life. 'Pillion? I'm not sure what you mean.'

Hettie patted the seat behind Bruiser. 'Up here. It's the only spare seat we have.'

Crestfallen and trying to control her temper, Lavender tried her famous bossy tactic. 'Miss Bagshot, I was hoping for the sidecar and it would make so much more sense for you to ride with Mr Venutius as you are more suitably dressed for it.'

'The trouble is that Tilly feels sick if I don't sit next to her in the sidecar. We have to sing to take her mind off it. You wouldn't want her breakfast all over that lovely dress, would you?'

Lavender gave in, hitched her dress up and clambered onto the back of the motorbike, and Hettie leapt in beside Tilly. Bruiser gave Miss Scarlet full throttle down the high street and the friends indulged in a full performance of the theme tune to *In the Kitchens and Up the Stairs*, while Lavender Stamp closed her eyes in terror and clung on for dear life.

CHAPTER THREE

Furcross House stood in a leafy area of the town where all the well-heeled cats made their homes. When Turner Page had sought approval to set up his library and community centre there, he had met with a certain amount of opposition from the residents of Sheba Gardens and the surrounding area. Most cats living in this pocket of affluence could afford to buy books and had no need to borrow them, and the thought of a community centre – bringing with it a certain sort of cat which had nothing in common with their values and principles – filled them with dread. Marcia Woolcoat had run a discreet operation at Furcross, providing a residential home for elderly cats who could afford her extortionate prices and who fitted in nicely – but Turner Page's vision of a centre where cats of all social levels could meet and enjoy all manner of cultural stimulation from books to beekeeping was a little wide of the mark.

There had been demonstrations, a high-profile campaign in the local paper, and a nasty incident involving the vandalism of Turner's library van, but the moment that Downton Tabby was announced as key speaker for the town's first literary festival all opposition to the library and community centre melted away in a puff of aristocatic smoke. The only gripe remaining was whether the good folk of Sheba Gardens should qualify for discounted rover tickets to the weekend's events. To reward the residents for all their efforts to have him evicted, Turner had decided against the discount and had passed it on to library and community centre groups instead.

When Bruiser swung Miss Scarlet into Sheba Gardens, it was clear that Downton Tabby's reception committee was gathering already and those who hadn't got tickets for the festival had turned out just to catch a glimpse of him.

'What a bloody nightmare,' grumbled Hettie as Bruiser brought the bike to a standstill outside the front door, narrowly missing the ticket tent which had been set up in the driveway.

Turner Page – resplendent in a bright yellow polka-dot bow tie and Fair Isle tank top – leapt down the steps to meet them and assisted Lavender Stamp onto firm ground while she did her utmost to protect her modesty. The floral-print dress has ridden up somewhat, and she struggled to conceal both her underwear and her embarrassment at being caught in such an ungainly situation. Turner attempted a greeting as Hettie and Tilly scrambled unaided from the sidecar, but it was clear that the festival director had well and truly lost his voice. Lavender staggered towards the ticket tent, still shaking from her biker experience and keen to get set up before the gates were opened at noon. Turner beckoned Hettie and Tilly to follow him into the house and Bruiser sped off on Miss Scarlet to continue with the Butters' festival catering deliveries.

Tilly was a regular visitor to Turner's library, as she devoured books and delighted in discovering new authors and their work. She had taken a keen interest in the alterations which had been made to accommodate a library and community centre into the old building, and knew her way around. Hettie hadn't come anywhere near the place since solving the famous Furcross case and, as Turner ushered them into the library, she marvelled at how light and airy the building now was, even in a heatwave. The walls were painted in reds and blues, embellished with countless paintings by kittens from the nursery which met there on Tuesdays; there were brightly coloured tables and chairs, large and small to cater for all age groups; and the bookshelves were packed with every conceivable category of reading that a cat's heart could desire.

Turner pointed to a desk in the centre of the room, where a short-haired ginger cat sat with his nose in a book. No one quite knew when Mr Anton Pushkin had turned up in the town. The fact that he'd come from Russia cloaked him in an air of mystery, but the one thing that was known about him was that he was inseparable from Turner Page, and the two cats shared a life full of books and exotic pullovers, interrupted only by the day-to-day concerns of running the library.

Tilly had met Mr Pushkin a number of times when he had stamped her books in and out of the library, and she nodded a greeting to him as she crossed to the desk with the red and blue lanyards.

'Ah, my dear Miss Tilly, we have been thrown together at last!' he said, clearing a space for the boxes and pulling another chair up for Tilly to sit on. 'My poor Turner has lost his voice, so I am to act in his place as the mouthpiece of authority. This desk is the powerhouse of the festival. All who carry the heavy burden of being intelligent enough to write a book must pass this way and be garlanded with the honour they deserve.'

Tilly stared down at Hettie's scribbled name tags, regarding them in a new light and wishing they'd spent a little more time over them, but she was pleased to be stationed with Mr Pushkin as she waited for her authors to arrive; she loved to hear him speak, regardless of what he was saying, and his accent delighted her.

Seeing that Tilly was nicely settled and noticing that Turner Page had wandered off into the garden to distribute the helpers' and stallholders' name tags, Hettie suddenly remembered that as well as being in charge of security for the weekend she was also now expected to come up with a pile of questions to fire at Downton Tabby. Security wasn't a problem – she had always planned to place herself on a deckchair between the library and the events marquee so that she could watch the comings and goings with as little effort as possible – but mugging up on the star of the festival had become a priority. She scanned the bookshelves, eventually finding a whole section on Downton Tabby, and grabbed several of his books before heading for the French windows to find a place in the sun where she could flick through his work and find some interesting topics to base her interview on.

Finding anywhere peaceful was clearly going to be impossible. The lawn leading to the marquee was bustling with stallholders, all keen to make their pitches as prominent as possible. Chapter and Spine, the booksellers from Southwool, had won the

31

franchise for the festival by heavily greasing Turner Page's paw with discounts on books for the library. They had taken up three trestle tables outside the events tent ready to catch the festivalgoers while their enthusiasm was at its peak. Tilly's friend, Jessie, was setting up a brightly painted wooden handcart to display her cloche hats and rainbow knits. Meridian Hambone, reputedly one of the oldest cats in the town, had adopted the no-frills approach which had always served her well in her high street hardware shop: she had laid her branded tote bags and T-shirts straight onto the grass and sat on an upturned galvanised bucket in the middle of them, chewing wine gums which she occasionally felt the need to spit out into a nearby flower bed.

Hettie's attention was drawn towards a stand-off between a prominent member of Cats of the Earth and a representative from Green Peas, a local vegetarian organisation. The issue appeared to be one of shade from the sun, and their allocated tables were pushed and shoved as they jockeyed for position. Secretly, Hettie hoped that Cats of the Earth would triumph as she had no time for those who only ate vegetables, but taking on the survival of the planet seemed equally bizarre on a hot, sunny day in the middle of a literary festival.

She moved away from the worthy area of stalls, looking for somewhere to read her Downton Tabby research, when Tilly emerged from the French windows, dragging a large holdall and hotly pursued by an attractive-looking cat with a shock of long blonde fur. Hettie noted that she was wearing a blue lanyard, which identified her as an author or publicist. The two cats headed for the marquee and Tilly relieved herself of her burden. Intrigued, Hettie approached in time to hear some unfortunate expletives from Mr Spine, who wasn't keen to share any of his retail space.

The blonde cat responded with a smile and proceeded to untie the holdall, which – to everyone's astonishment – popped up to form a three-sided stall complete with roof and shelf for merchandise. There was no need for Hettie to glance at the name tag; she knew instantly that standing before her was the celebrated crime writer Nicolette Upstart, oozing charm and standing her ground with the bookstall.

Mr Pushkin was next out of the French windows, balancing three large boxes which he brought to a crash landing next to the pop-up. Grateful and still smiling, Nicolette proceeded to unpack her stock while Tilly looked on in delight, noticing several copies of the author's latest book, *London Drains and Other Grimes*. Next came tote bags, fridge magnets, mugs, bandanas, signed photographs and a rather lovely range of day-glow bookmarks, all sporting the titles of previous books. The striped pop-up stall would be the talk of the festival and the envy of any author whose publishers hadn't quite got the hang of getting their books into bookshops. Nicolette's success as a bestselling author was not only down to her masterly storytelling but to her tenacity in going out to meet her readers, offering them the highest quality merchandise to remember her by. Tilly clapped her paws in delight as more treasures emerged from the boxes, and she'd quite forgotten her post as meeter and greeter until Mr Pushkin shouted from the French windows that P. D. Hodge had arrived. Leaving Nicolette brushing her long blonde fur, ready to meet her public, Tilly returned to the library to welcome Polly Hodge.

Hettie slunk round the edge of the marquee and found herself a peaceful spot at the entrance to the memorial gardens, positioning herself in close proximity to the hospitality tent, where an endless supply of the Butter sisters' delights would be on offer throughout the two days. She squinted against the sun, looking for the clock on the old hospital block to her left, remembering her first room search there during the Furcross case. A lot had happened since then: several murders, a number of thefts and an assortment of petty crimes had come to the door of her detective agency, all solved and tucked away in the town's more lurid history. She was proud of what she and Tilly had achieved in such a short time, and – with help from her friends Bruiser and Poppa – the No. 2 Feline Detective

Agency had become a surprising success. No one was more surprised than Hettie herself.

She opened the first of Downton Tabby's books, going straight to the 'about the author' section, and her heart sank as she noticed that his biographical credits ran to eight pages before the book even started. Public school, sporting genius, scholar, captain of industry, conservationist of baronial mansions, OBE, CBE, Knight of the Garter, author, film director, screenwriter and the creator of the nation's top TV show for the last five years, winning three Bluster awards and two lifetime achievements, which Hettie found a little odd as he was only in his middle years.

The smell of bacon drifted out from the hospitality tent, followed by a loud crash of crockery. It took Hettie no time at all to deduce that the all-day breakfast was on its way and that Delirium Treemints had begun her shift on beverages. Delirium was known for her nerves; she lived on them and by them, but was always ready to step forward to dispense tea and coffee at the drop of a hat – or, in her case, a whole tea set. The craze for plastic and melamine had significantly improved her performance at functions, but there was still cause for concern over the spilt milk, tea and fruit juice, even if the crockery now bounced.

Hettie decided to give up on her Downton Tabby research. The job was easy. There was nothing he hadn't done in his life, and she knew enough about the TV show to busk her way through the event, so she decided to apply an old trick which she used on songs she didn't want to sing in her music days: start it off, and let the audience do the rest.

She strode back to the library to return the books, noticing that the festival was now in full swing. The floodgates had clearly been opened and a vision of Lavender Stamp being trampled to death in the stampede entered her head, but she pushed the thought away as uncharitable. The library was buzzing with cats, all clambering to get a front row seat for the first event – an intimate crime fiction workshop with Polly Hodge. P. D. Hodge had held the title of Queen of Crime since the demise of Agatha Crispy. Her dark psychological thrillers had been at the top of the book charts for years and her publishers, Flavour and Flavour, allowed her the time and space between books, knowing that they would always have a bestseller on their paws when she delivered a new one. She had travelled far and wide and was adored all over the world, mostly on expensive cruise liners where eager cats would queue up to share the captain's table with her.

Even Hettie approved of Polly Hodge, as she was known locally. She had a fiercely intelligent mind, which she shared with the readers of the *Sunday Snout* on a regular basis, and her murder plots were acts of genius. Even Tilly, who solved most fictional cases long before the dénouement, had been regularly stumped by Polly's solutions. She was indeed a master of crime. With rare admiration, Hettie looked across to the corner of the library where Polly was gathering her flock around her. She was a sight to behold – a white, bespectacled cat, looking every bit the favourite grandmother as she encouraged her audience to come closer, but Hettie knew that beneath the sweet old cat veneer lurked a mind capable of the most horrific and spiteful murders ever to be written down in a work of fiction. In her brief and recent experience of catching real murderers, Hettie had found them invariably to be pillars of the community – just like Polly Hodge, in fact.

'Mr Pushkin is holding the fort for a bit,' said Tilly, as Hettie forced Downton Tabby's books back into the 'T' section. 'We could go and get some food if you like? The Brontës aren't due for another hour and Polly Hodge is just starting up, so she won't need anything for a bit.'

'That's the best idea you've had all day. We need to discuss our strategy.'

'Why? Are you expecting trouble?' Tilly looked a little concerned.

'No, not really, but I thought you could let me know when your breaks will be so we can meet up in hospitality. Judging by the amount of baking the

Butters have been doing, I think that tent will be the highlight of my festival.'

Tilly giggled as the two friends fought their way through the stalls. Meridian Hambone seemed to be doing a roaring trade with her T-shirts; Hettie noticed that there was a growing band of festivalgoers sporting the 'Littertray Festival' slogan across their chests as they abandoned their plain outfits to get into the swing of things. Nicolette Upstart's head bandanas were proving popular, too, as the longer haired cats were feeling the full force of the midday heat. It was no surprise to see only a small clutch of pale, skinny cats gathered around the Green Peas stall, and the Cats of the Earth had no takers at all, sitting dejected and sunburnt in their own patch of global warming.

Hettie made a beeline for the events marquee. 'Come on, it'll be quicker if we go straight through here,' she said, tugging Tilly along by her yellow T-shirt. The marquee was cool and empty and smelt of newly mown grass. The stage was set up at one end and furnished with a table and two chairs, and the rest of the space was taken up with a multitude of chairs and benches laid out in neat rows with an aisle running down the middle. Hettie was instantly transported back to her days on the road, when music festivals were bread and butter to her band. She loved an empty tent, so full of anticipation; for her, it was a time to gather her thoughts in peace and silence before the fans transformed the space into a throbbing hubbub of noise and colour. She missed those days, but had been sensible enough to know that the adage of leaving them wanting more when you were at the top of your game was a master stroke of good marketing. Her records had doubled in price since she had hung up her guitar; it was better to be a legend than a has-been, and she'd sat through plenty of those.

The reality of being on the road suddenly hit her squarely between the eyes as she and Tilly moved to the backstage area of the marquee, intent on passing out into the sunshine where the hospitality tent was only yards away. Before they could reach it, the rear exit was barged open by a round table on wheels with an assortment of swords, helmets and cloaks piled on top of it. 'Oops!' came the apologetic comment as Hettie and Tilly flung themselves to the side to avoid the full force of the table. Muddy Fryer made her entrance, hot and bothered and dragging a large red suitcase behind her, having given her round table a hearty shove into the marquee. 'I've left the van on the cricket field – I hope that's OK,' she said, wiping the sweat off her face with the hem of her skirt. 'I thought I'd get me stuff in before the first event. I think I'm on at seven before Downton Tabby.'

Tilly nodded, looking a little star-struck, and Hettie went instantly into gig mode, although she too loved

Muddy's music and wished it didn't have to be diluted by books. 'Let me help,' she said, steering the round table into a suitable space at the back of the stage. 'We'll get some help later for your set-up. There's an hour between Nicolette Upstart and you so you'll have loads of time for a soundcheck.'

Muddy appreciated the information but had more pressing concerns. 'Have you got a merch table so I can lay out me stuff? I'm only here for today so I need to get selling. I'll be off like a rocket after Downton Tabby, as I'm doing the Clogs and Sods Fest tomorrow with the Tollpiddle Martyrs and it's a hell of a drive from here.'

Tilly came to the rescue, putting her shyness to one side. 'My friend, Jessie, might have room on her stall if you'd like to follow me? She does rainbow knits and cloches.'

Muddy took up her suitcase and followed Tilly across the marquee. Hettie wasted no time in joining the queue now forming in the hospitality tent, where she ordered two all-day breakfasts. The tent was a sight to behold and as Hettie waited impatiently to be served she marvelled at the facilities that had been laid on for the helpers and the so-called artists. In her festival days, you were lucky to be given a space in a wigwam to change into your stage clothes, let alone a tent piled high with every pie, pastry and breakfast bap a cat could desire. There was also a complete field kitchen for cooking hot food. The Butters had thought of everything, including segregation to give the festival stars a brief respite from prying eyes while they ate their food. Hettie surveyed the seating areas: one section held several long trestle tables and fold-up chairs and was signposted 'Staff and Helpers' Canteen'. The other was smaller and partitioned off with giant palms supplied by Prune and Pots, the town's garden centre. Hettie could see that this area had tables laid up with clean white tablecloths and comfortable high-backed chairs. She smiled to herself, knowing from her own experience that artists were probably the messiest visitors to any festival; fame and fortune often bred a bohemian attitude to social graces, and those white tablecloths were in for a bit of a hammering.

Tilly entered the tent a few minutes later with the glad tidings that Jessie and Muddy were getting on like a house on fire, and that there had already been brisk business on Muddy's records and tapes. The breakfasts arrived at the same time and the two cats pounced on them as if they hadn't eaten for a week. With an additional egg stain on her T-shirt, which she hoped no one would notice, Tilly wiped her mouth with the back of her paw as Hettie wiped both their plates clean with her final piece of toast. Sitting back on her chair, she took up the table menu, ready to discuss their next meal when Poppa rushed into the tent looking nothing like his usual calm self. Tilly waved and he rushed over to them.

'Thank goodness I've found you,' he said, eyeing up the empty plates with a look of sad disappointment. 'All hell has kicked off in the car park. The Brontë sisters have turned up in their camper van and are insisting on parking it backstage. I've told them it's the cricket field or nothing, but they won't have it and they're asking to speak to someone in charge.'

Both Poppa and Hettie looked at Tilly, waiting for a response which – considering the urgency of the situation – took some time. She pulled a notepad out of her shoulder bag and consulted one of the pages. 'Well, there's nothing down in my notes about a camper van. They're staying in the old hospital block – one share and one single, and they're lucky to have that as Downton Tabby is taking up three rooms all to himself. Where are they at the moment?'

'Sitting in the camper outside the main door, trading insults with Lavender Stamp,' said Poppa, looking wistfully towards the food counter.

Hettie was considering whether the camper van was a security issue which needed her attention when Mr Pushkin made a dramatic entrance through the tent flap and headed straight for Tilly. 'My dear, you must come quick or I fear murder will be done! The Brontë sisters have set about Miss Stamp and we are in need of first aid.'

Hettie, Tilly and Poppa abandoned the hospitality tent, pausing only to grab Bruiser, who was unloading another batch of pies from Miss Scarlet's sidecar.

'Come on, this should be worth seeing!' cried Hettie as they pushed their way through the stalls and back into the library, racing past P. D. Hodge's crime workshop and out into the driveway of Furcross House. The scene was one of carnage. Lavender Stamp stood next to a hand-painted lime green camper van, swaying in the heat and clutching a large wad of cotton wool to her nose to prevent the blood from making any further impression on her flower-print dress. Hilary and Cherry Fudge stood by her side, sporting their first-aid sashes and ready to provide further assistance as and when required.

The Brontë sisters were lined up in front of Lavender like three tall skittles, all goading the postmistress into further conflict. The cat in the middle seemed to be the leader and was certainly the most audible of the three, giving a masterclass in expressive language. 'Don't think getting haughty taughty with us will butter any parsnips. We'll park our van where we like and there's nothing you can do to stop us. We don't take orders from the likes of you. We are from Porkshire, where we eat cats like you for our dinner. And if you need another slap, one of my sisters here is happy to oblige.' The other two Brontës moved forward as one at their sibling's bidding.

Entertaining as the spectacle was, Hettie decided to intervene, trying a charm offensive to defuse the situation while Tilly hid behind her. 'Welcome to our literary festival. Please follow me into the library where we can issue you with your security passes before taking you over to the hospitality tent for lunch. If you would care to leave your luggage and the key to your camper, we will find a nice space for it close to the accommodation block where you are staying.'

Bruiser, Poppa and Tilly all stared in admiration at Hettie's tact and diplomacy as the three Brontë sisters moved towards the door of Furcross House, offering beaming smiles to the fans who had gathered to greet them. Lavender Stamp shrank away to her ticket tent to ponder on the thought that one day her dictatorial attitude might get her something much more serious than a bloody nose.

The Brontës lined up to receive their blue lanyards, which Mr Pushkin placed around their necks. The sisters were so alike that there was a little confusion as to who was who, but eventually Charlene, Emmeline and Ann had been paired off with the correct name tags and all was calm, at least for the moment. Bruiser and Poppa took it upon themselves to move the camper van to a spot behind the accommodation block and deposit the luggage outside the authors' allotted rooms. Hettie and Tilly escorted their charges through the crowd to the hospitality tent, where they left them eating their way through the menu. Relieved to have averted the first potential crisis, they returned to the peace and quiet of the empty marquee.

Tilly sat down on the edge of the stage looking more than a little upset. 'I'm not cut out for all of this,' she said, allowing a stray tear to fall from the end of her nose. 'I was so excited when Turner Page asked me to book the authors, and it was lovely going to visit other festivals to see what they had to offer. I thought everyone would be like Polly Hodge. She's such a nice cat, even though she's famous.'

'But that's the point,' said Hettie. 'She's got nothing more to prove, so she can afford to be nice. From what I've seen of the Brontës, they're like fish out of water. That sort of cat is as hard as nails, but deep down they're the same as all the rest, pushing their books and trying to make a name for themselves. I think by the time Downton Tabby puts in an appearance, the Brontës will have been cut down to size. Let's face it, just about every cat who's bought a ticket for this weekend has bought it to see him. Any other author is just a bonus. Come on, cheer up. Why don't you go and treat yourself to something from Nicolette's pop-up? She's nice and she hasn't caused any trouble.'

Tilly brightened at the prospect of some retail therapy and left Hettie choosing a deckchair in which to have a power nap in the sun before things got underway in the events tent. On her way out into the sunshine, she checked the running order pinned to the tent flap, noting that Charlene Brontë would be kicking off the proceedings, followed by Nicolette Upstart, Muddy Fryer and then Downton Tabby. Furcross Convention, the house band, was due to bring day one to a conclusion, providing that none of them had withered away in the heat. They were all of an age where a walking frame would be more useful than a guitar, but it would be Turner Page's big moment as he had appointed himself drummer and percussionist.

CHAPTER FOUR

Charlene Brontë sat pulling threads in the white tablecloth as her sisters poked the final pieces of a Butters' vanilla slice into their mouths. The sisters had come a long way since the days of sitting round their kitchen table at home, making up stories to amuse themselves with their brother Bonville. Their childhood winters, spent in the draughty old parsonage above the mill town of Teethly, were long and relentless. Bonville had suffered the most and had taken to his bed with a liquid catnip habit that had eventually destroyed him, which was a shame as he did paint a nice picture when he was in the mood.

Charlene had had to assume responsibility

for the running of the home from a very young age after her mother died from ginger beer on the lungs, a nasty disease which was prevalent in the moorland areas of Porkshire due to the lack of fresh water and the abundance of ginger beer plants. Her father, a direct descendant of the famous family, had invested in the old parsonage when it came onto the market unexpectedly due to a feud between old and new members of the Brontë Society. The old Brontës, as they were known, had lived and died in the parsonage, leaving their unfinished manuscripts behind the fireplace in the dining room. Many years later, the work had been discovered while a back boiler was being fitted and Charlene, Emmeline and Ann had been encouraged by their father to finish the books and become authors in their own right.

Their path to success had been a difficult one, especially as their father had recently gone quite mad and now spent his days taking potshots with a home-made catapult at any cat who came near the parsonage. Charlene had almost single-handedly raised her sisters in her own image. The only difference was the books they'd been given to work on. Emmeline had a talent for poetry and it had taken Charlene all her time to convince her sister that rhymes didn't sell, especially the grim old ones that Emmeline turned out. Not a laugh to be had.

Ann was different: she just did as she was told and found much joy in being part of anything at all.

It had been a great surprise to the good cats of Teethly when Emmeline's book, *Withering Sights*, topped the bestseller list for a fortnight, outstripping Charlene's *Jane Hair* and leaving Ann's effort, *The Tomcat of Wildfell Hall*, in the slush pile on the desk of Penny Stone-Cragg, their agent in the north. To lift her fortunes and to improve on her now dwindling sales, Charlene had spearheaded a festival tour, hoping to gain more exposure for herself whilst coining it in with Emmeline's paperback and a rather hurried autobiography which Ann had published herself and which was doing rather well in the independent bookshops. Charlene had harboured hopes of seeing *Jane Hair* hit the TV screens, but so far it had been spurned by producers and screenwriters alike. In fact, Penny Stone-Cragg had given up on proffering it any further, so abusive were the rejection slips which the bonnet drama was receiving.

The camper van which had caused so much trouble earlier was their own special bit of independence and the last visible sign of their brother Bonville, who had dragged himself off his deathbed to decorate it the day before he died. The fact that he'd embellished the paintwork with a number of indecent depictions from Greek legends had completely passed his sisters by in their keenness to break out into the wider world of art and literature under their own steam. The camper had also given Emmeline an independence of her own, as she was the only Brontë sister capable of driving it.

Tilly, wearing a new bandana, poked her head round the hospitality tent flap. Seeing that the Brontës were gathered en masse, she approached in the hope that food and a nice sit-down had mellowed them. 'I wonder if you would like to see your rooms?' she asked, addressing the lanyard called Charlene.

Charlene beamed back at her and the three sisters stood together, waiting for direction. Tilly was pleased not to get too involved with any further conversation and led the way out of the tent and across to the old hospital block, now a temporary home for the authors who needed to stay overnight at the festival. She could see as she entered the building that Poppa and Bruiser had dropped the Brontës' bags off outside the relevant doors; all she needed to do was point her paw in the right direction and beat a hasty retreat.

But Ann scuppered things by making it clear that she had no intention of sharing with Emmeline. 'I've shared with her all me life and I'll not spend another night listening to her sad old poems,' she wailed.

'They're all about being buried in the snow and it's twenty-eight degrees out there today. I bet the nights round here aren't a deal cooler.'

Emmeline looked fragile after her sister's outburst and Charlene – whilst agreeing with Ann's comments regarding the poetry – decided to calm troubled waters. 'I'll tell thee what we'll do – we'll put Emmeline in the room on her own and I'll share with you, Ann.'

Tilly watched as Emmeline crumpled further and slumped down on her suitcase. 'I am fearful of being on my own in such a strange place with not even the moor to bring me comfort.'

Charlene licked her lips nervously. 'Now come on, stop this nonsense. I've told you not to keep going on about the moor in front of company. Save it for your presentation tomorrow. Folks won't mind if you go off on one when you're talking about Katty and Heatclip. You'll have to share with me, and that way I can keep an eye on you.'

With that, Charlene and Emmeline gathered their bags and let themselves into their room. Ann did the same and suddenly all was quiet, and Tilly retraced her footsteps in time to join Hettie for a tea and cake session before the much-awaited arrival of Downton Tabby.

The tea tent was busy and Hettie had bagged a table close to the exit to avoid getting stuck with over-enthusiastic authors wanting to sing their own praises over a fresh cream slice. It occurred to her that writing a book gave those particular creatures licence to bore any passing cat to death with their opinions, and, as more authors arrived, they seemed to form little cliques. The biographers sat at one table, arguing, while the romantic novelists stood out as overweight, highly decorated females, competitive in their bid to wear the brightest lipstick and the most luridly painted claws. The exponents of crime fiction seemed to be the most normal of the gathering. Hettie noticed that Nicolette Upstart and Polly Hodge were enjoying a high tea in the company of Sandy McPaw-Spitt, who had dropped in to do a signing for his latest book. There was much laughter coming from their table, and the salmon turnovers and chocolate wedge cake left only crumbs as evidence. She marvelled at their sunny dispositions, knowing that they all embraced the art of murder in their day jobs.

'Ooh, is that cream horn for me?' asked Tilly, spotting her friend amid a sea of fans looking for autographs.

Hettie nodded and Tilly slumped down on the chair next to her, fanning herself with the menu card. 'I'm so hot and bothered. I think my ears have caught the sun – they've gone red.'

Hettie laughed. 'Well, get tucked into your cake.

You can always stick some of the cream on your ears if there's any left. Have the Brontës settled into their accommodation?'

Tilly's response was slightly muffled through a mouthful of flaky pastry. 'They *are* a nightmare – sibling rivalry barely does it justice. I feel very sorry for Emmeline. The other two are really nasty to her about her poems.'

'I thought she was the one who wrote *Withering Sights*? That's not poetry, is it?'

Tilly shook her head, spraying fresh cream across her whiskers and down one side of Hettie's T-shirt. 'No, but I think she *prefers* to write poetry, and she's got this thing about the moor.'

'The more what?' asked Hettie, slightly irritated by the heat.

Tilly giggled. 'No, not "more what". *The* moor. According to the back of Ann Brontë's autobiography, her sister is obsessed with the moor where they live and wanders about on it all day in a thin cotton dress and socks, shouting out her poems.'

'Well she's obviously barking mad. And if she prefers poetry, why has she written a huge book that's only fit for propping a door open?'

'*Withering Sights* was started by one of her ancestors and Emmeline finished it. It's become a bestseller and has made her lots and lots of

53

money. She's much more successful than her sisters. Charlene's *Jane Hair* got panned by the critics. One of them called it "an out-of-date, rambling bit of Victorian nonsense".'

'What's it about then?' asked Hettie, trying not to sound too interested.

Tilly thought for a moment. 'It's hard to say exactly. I only got halfway through it. Once I realised that there weren't going to be any good murders, I lost interest. It's mainly about a mad cat they keep in the attic who can't be trusted with matches.'

Tilly's appraisal of *Jane Hair* was interrupted by the gushing approach of Bugs Anderton, president of the town's Friendship Club. 'Brace yourself,' muttered Hettie, as the tall ginger cat made swift progress towards their table.

'Miss Bagshot! How pleased I am to find you in such a crush. I've not seen the like since my annual trip to the Highland Games!'

Bugs Anderton was proud of her Scottish origins and never needed an excuse to refer to them. Her qualities lay in her organisational skills, which were guaranteed to put fear into any community, and Hettie had chosen her to escort Downton Tabby at the festival because she was one of the few cats who could be relied upon not to be seduced by his celebrity status. Bugs had formed an unlikely friendship with Hettie and Tilly, based on a tide of gratitude; not long ago, they had saved her life in a vicious murder case which still reverberated around the town.

'I am here for my security briefing,' she announced, pulling up a chair and sweeping the tent with her eyes until she located Delirium Treemints. Having made eye contact, Delirium seemed to go into overdrive: without any further communication, she loaded a tray with a stacked tea and began her journey across the tent. In her haste to please, she slipped on a stray pork pie and slid several yards before coming to an ungainly halt at Polly Hodge's table. A mini sardine quiche escaped from the stacked tea and fixed itself to Polly's tabard top, where she unwittingly wore it for the rest of the day. Delirium gathered herself in a flurry of apologies and continued her progress to Hettie's table, delivering the tea almost intact to a round of applause from the romantic novelists, who all loved a happy ending.

Delirium melted away into the background for some gentle pairing of cups and saucers, while Hettie began her very brief briefing. 'I think the main problem with Downton Tabby is his own opinion of himself,' she said, 'so I think you should treat it more as a personal assistant role than a security job.' Bugs nodded enthusiastically and started on the second layer of her stacked tea. 'The important thing is that we keep him happy and give him anything he asks for.'

In the absence of Delirium, Bugs poured her own tea and stirred four lumps of sugar into it, looking thoughtful. 'If I might raise one or two issues at this point? Mr Downton Tabby is rarely off the front pages of the tabloids, and he's always being pooped by someone.'

Hettie looked confused and Tilly came to the rescue. 'I think you mean "papped", as in paparazzi.'

'Exactly so,' continued Bugs. 'How will I protect him from the more aggressive fans should they surge forward en masse with their cameras and their autograph books? He's surely the "must-have" photograph of the weekend.'

'We've got that one covered,' responded Hettie. 'We're bringing him in round the back. He'll be in his Rolls-Royce when he arrives and we've got the back car park cordoned off except for the Brontës' camper, which shouldn't be a problem, so he won't even meet the public until his event later on. Tilly's organised a book signing and photo opportunity for tomorrow with Chapter and Spine. His agent says he'll only pose for cats who buy his books, so it'll be a bit of a scrum, but we'll be there to help with Poppa and Bruiser as back-up.'

Even Hettie had to admit that her plans were beginning to sound like a proper security job, but nobody could have predicted the events that were to follow later that evening. The photos which would be taken the next day would present a much more macabre image of the festival's top celebrity, and Prunella Snap and Hacky Redtop from the town's local paper would have another exclusive on their paws.

CHAPTER FIVE

Refreshed from their afternoon tea, Hettie and Tilly fought their way through the crowds to clear a path for Bugs Anderton, who looked increasingly as if she might collapse from heatstroke. Downton Tabby was due at any moment and they needed to be in position when his Rolls-Royce swung through the gates of Furcross House, if only to deter Lavender Stamp from challenging him about parking.

They cut through the events marquee, where a small crowd was gathering to bag the best view of Charlene Brontë. The stalls area was buzzing with bookaholics, all grabbing copies of the festival authors' books and hoping to be first in the queue to have them signed. *Jane Hair* was selling one or two copies, but Emmeline and Ann Brontë's books were moving at a brisk pace and Chapter and Spine had laid on a magnificent display for Downton Tabby which took up half of their allotted tables.

Hettie's attention was suddenly drawn to an altercation which seemed to be coming from the front of the bookstall.

'You lot couldn't market a balm cake in a sandwich shop! How come he's got half the bloody space and the rest of us are reduced to a neat pile hanging off the end?' The dulcet tones of Charlene Brontë rang out and Hettie – remembering Lavender Stamp's bloody nose – burrowed through the crowd to see if she could help. Tilly and Bugs continued on to the library where Mr Pushkin was nervously pacing the floor, waiting for news of the star turn's arrival.

By the time Hettie reached the front of the bookstall, the situation had escalated and all three Brontë sisters were pitching in. Downton Tabby's books were flying through the air to make way for the Porkshire trio's efforts, and Mr Chapter was powerless to stop the assault on his stock. Mr Spine cowered under one of the tables, hoping that things would eventually calm down, but Charlene and her sisters still had much to say on the subject of product placement. The crowd was loving the spectacle and cheered the Brontës on as the sisters played to their audience.

'These book festivals are bread and margarine to

us,' declared Charlene. 'Downton Tabby has more money than he could ever spend. For him, selling books is small change in his fat back pocket. It's our books that need displaying – we've travelled a long way for this and our camper doesn't run on fresh air.'

She leapt up onto the book table to address the crowd, and Hettie stared in dismay at the mob rule which was building. Suddenly, inspiration struck. She nudged the thin, grey-striped cat standing next to her and whispered in her ear, watching as her message was passed on; the crowd began to thin out and move away from the bookstall, depriving the Brontë sisters of their audience. Thinking it safe at last, Mr Spine emerged from under the table to join his partner, who was gathering up the Downton Tabby stock from the ground where it had landed in the dust. Hettie offered her paw to Charlene as she clambered down from the book table, looking slightly less embarrassed than her sisters. 'It's lovely and cool backstage in the events marquee,' she said. 'Perhaps you'd like to compose yourself there before your event? And I'm sure your sisters will want a front row seat to listen to you.' Charlene nodded, giving a hint of a smile, and Emmeline and Ann followed her into the tent after putting the finishing touches to a display of their own books.

Mr Chapter, pleased to see the back of the Brontës as they disappeared into the marquee, came round

61

to the front of his stall to try and repair some of the chaos. Knowing that he would aggravate the situation further if he touched the sisters' new display, he piled the other authors' books around them, limiting the Downton Tabby arrangement to half its former glory.

As Hettie walked away to catch up with Tilly and Bugs, she couldn't help but sympathise with Charlene's comments. Downton Tabby was beginning to get on her nerves and she hadn't even met him yet, let alone shared a platform with him as she would soon be required to do. She smiled to herself as she passed the Green Peas stall, where a massive queue was forming. The rumour she had started in the book scrum had paid off, as Downton's fans waited patiently for him to put in an appearance. As with most rumours there was no substance to it, but the cats running the vegetarian stall were pleased to have the company of the crowd.

When she arrived at the library, she was pleased to see that it was a hive of peaceful activity. There was a kitten's reading group hosted by J. K. Roll-on, an up-and-coming author who famously wrote her books in her local Chinese takeaway; tucked away in the corner usually reserved for newspapers, the fantasy writer Terry Scratchit was holding court with his followers, who all seemed to be dressed in cloaks and wide-brimmed hats, a fashion statement made popular by the author himself; and the festival band had taken over the cookery and leisure section of the library as a dressing room and were quietly changing strings and tuning up their instruments. All sported a 'Littertray Festival' T-shirt, suggesting that Meridian Hambone had been doing a roaring trade. There was, however, no sign of the drummer and it occurred to Hettie that Turner Page, the festival director, hadn't put in an appearance since they arrived; so far, he had played no part in the direction of the festival in any way and seemed to have disappeared without a trace.

Tilly and Bugs Anderton had joined Mr Pushkin at his desk and they were all pacing round it like participants in some obscure satanic ritual. With Downton Tabby expected at any minute, their excitement had reached fever pitch.

'I think we'd better go and wait by the gates,' said Hettie, interrupting their progress. 'He's due round about now.' She reached into the box of blue lanyards and located the correct name tag. 'I doubt he'll need this as it's obvious who he is, but we should try and stick to the plan.' Bugs and Tilly nodded and followed Hettie out of Furcross House, leaving Mr Pushkin to his pacing.

The driveway was relatively clear, but beyond the gates in Sheba Gardens the crowds who hadn't bought a ticket for the festival were three-deep all along the approach. Some cats waved flags, others had banners and all sweltered in the heat. Greasy Tom had taken advantage of the situation by parking his fast-food van at the bottom of the road, and was busy supplying sustenance to the crowd who had been gathering since six o'clock that morning.

'I hope he's on time,' said Hettie. 'Charlene Brontë's about to start her event and we need to keep an eye on that one. God knows what she'll come out with next, and her sisters are just as bad.'

Tilly agreed, feeling a little guilty at having booked them in the first place. 'They were offering a three for two and we were running out of budget, so I thought it would be a good idea to bring in some northern culture,' she admitted, adding in her own defence: 'And Emmeline does have a bestseller.'

'So you keep telling me, but it doesn't change the fact that all three of them have been a pile of bloody trouble since they got here.'

Bugs decided to join in, being a closet Brontë fan. 'I find Emmeline's poetry quite remarkable,' she said. 'Her connection with the natural elements is quite unique. You can smell the heather and feel the rain on your face in some of her work.'

'When she's not slinging mud at you,' interrupted Hettie.

'Ah, but it's the passion that beats in her breast, Miss Bagshot. The moor is her life. She *is* the moor.'

Hettie backed away from Bugs, fearing that she might lapse into one of Emmeline's poems at any moment. Tilly licked her lips nervously and stared out of the gates, hoping to summon up a Rolls-Royce to save them from any further discussion on the Brontës, for whom she was beginning to feel entirely responsible.

They didn't wait long. Suddenly the crowd lining the route erupted into spontaneous applause and cheering as a bright yellow Rolls-Royce came into view, making slow and deliberate progress along Sheba Gardens towards the gates of Furcross House. Lavender Stamp emerged from her ticket tent to add to the welcoming committee, and Hettie was relieved to see that she had sponged most of the blood off her floral-print sundress. She was flanked on either side by Hilary and Cherry Fudge, standing by in case their first-aid services were required once again.

The driver of the Rolls-Royce halted at the gates and Hettie gave Bugs Anderton a push in the direction of the car. 'Do your welcome stuff as quickly as you can,' she whispered. 'Tilly and I will walk the car into the parking space, so whatever you do, don't let him get out of the car or we'll have a riot on our hands.'

For once in her autocratic life, Bugs did as she was told and approached the car, but she was hauled into the back of the Rolls by a reddish brown paw before she had even managed to utter the second welcome in her usual canon of three, reserved for high office dignitaries. Hettie nodded to the driver, inviting him to follow her as she led the way through to the car park at the back of the old hospital block, and Tilly followed on reluctantly, knowing that she would have to conquer her shyness long enough to show Downton Tabby to the rooms she had allocated for his stay. Nobody gave a second thought to what was happening in the back seat of the Rolls-Royce, but it would be safe to say that Bugs Anderton was slightly more worldly-wise when she fell out onto the tarmac, looking a little dishevelled and blushing from her ginger ears to her ginger toes.

The chauffeur, having assisted Bugs out of the car, moved round to the other side to release his master who stepped out looking every bit the millionaire celebrity. To say that he would stand out in a crowd was a massive understatement: his bright orange-and-yellow-checked suit, complete with waistcoat and spats, suggested an aristocat whom time or fashion had never bothered. If he hadn't been such a superstar, some would say he was fat. His reddy brown fur was slicked down on his head, producing a parting between his ears, and his whiskers were waxed within an inch of their lives, standing out from his face as if they had arrived separately. The look was completed to perfection by a black silver-topped cane and a monocle which hung around his neck.

Both Tilly and Hettie stood for a moment with their mouths open; the anticipation of the superstar's arrival had been nothing compared to the reality of his presence. Bugs Anderton recovered herself sufficiently to offer some introductions. 'Sir Downton, if I may introduce you to Miss Hettie Bagshot, our head of security, and Miss Matilda Jenkins, our author coordinator.'

Hettie bowed, not knowing what else to do, and Tilly didn't respond at all; it had been several years since she'd heard her full name spoken and she had quite forgotten what it sounded like.

Downton Tabby nodded and stood waiting for further direction from the reception committee, swinging back on his heels. As none was forthcoming, Bugs Anderton came to the rescue and defused the rather awkward situation by moving things along. 'If you would care to follow Miss Jenkins, she will be pleased to show you to your accommodation. I would then be delighted to offer you some light refreshment in our hospitality area.'

Tilly stepped forward as the chauffeur unloaded a number of suitcases out of the boot of the Rolls-Royce, handing two of the heaviest ones to Hettie. The party made its way into the accommodation block, where Tilly opened up three of the rooms. One had been made into a pleasant sitting room, filled with the best furniture borrowed from Turner Page's own quarters, and the other two were bedrooms which had been hurriedly redecorated and still smelt of emulsion paint.

'And where will you be staying, my dear lady?' asked the celebrity. 'Our brief encounter in my Rolls-Royce must surely be the beginning of a wonderful weekend, full of promise.'

Bugs Anderton was flattered by his remarks but knew she would have to get a grip before her reputation lay in tatters around her. She had read widely about Downton Tabby's amorous adventures and had even found herself daydreaming about what it would be like to become one of them, but she had a job to do.

Satisfied that Bugs had everything under control, except perhaps her pulse rate, Hettie and Tilly backed away from the festival's star and made their way back to the events tent, where Charlene Brontë was reading a passage from *Jane Hair* to a captivated audience, even though the microphone was somewhat intermittent. Her sisters sat on the front row, looking bored and fidgeting with their lanyards.

'All peaceful in here,' whispered Hettie. 'Time for an ice cream?'

Tilly nodded enthusiastically and the two friends headed for the tea tent, leaving Charlene in raptures over her own novel and the audience in raptures over Charlene.

Two vanilla tubs and a strawberry Mivvi later, Hettie and Tilly returned to the marquee in time to hear the dying moments of Nicolette Upstart's presentation.

She was revealing some of the more lurid details of the research she had undertaken to create the perfect murder, and received a standing ovation started by Polly Hodge, who had been sitting on the front row. As the author left the stage, there was a stampede towards the book tables and Nicolette darted round the back of the tent in time to execute her pop-up stall and cash in on the crowd's enthusiasm.

The marquee was suddenly peaceful again. There was an hour's break before Muddy Fryer gave her performance and Hettie and Tilly sat on the edge of the stage, awaiting her arrival to help with her soundcheck. 'It's a strange business, all this book stuff,' said Hettie, thinking out loud. 'These cats spend their days writing about the worst things imaginable, making up the nastiest murders as if it were some sort of competitive sport. I wonder how they'd react if they had a real murder to deal with? And then there are the Brontës – what's that all about? Pushing themselves at every possible opportunity, descending on us like harpies from hell and competing with each other to sell the most books. And as for Downton Tabby – he's like a character straight out of his own TV series. A bumbling upper-class twit, really, with an air of his own importance that might strangle him one day.'

Tilly giggled at Hettie's assessment of the festival participants so far. 'I think you're being a bit harsh,' she said. 'There are so many books out there to choose from and, if you're an author, you've got to promote them whenever you can – that's what these festivals are for. And every festival needs a Downton Tabby or no one would come.'

Hettie thought for a moment about Tilly's logic, then waded in. 'If you need to go to such extremes to promote the books, why write them in the first place? Every cat you meet these days seems to think they have a book in them, and judging by the state of the Brontës' camper van, there's no money in it. Writing a book is a self-indulgence that everyone else is expected to pay for, and when you've bought and read the book, what use is it? I admit that Downton Tabby attracts a good crowd, but by the time Turner Page has paid all the costs involved in putting the festival on, he'll be lucky to have enough left to reseed his lawn after the whole town has tramped across it.'

Tilly was about to discuss the importance of community events when Muddy Fryer made a somewhat unusual entrance through the tent flap at the back of the stage. She seemed to be wearing a pair of wings and a hood with a bright orange beak protruding from it. Alarmed at the vision before her, Hettie moved to help as Muddy – unable to see where she was going – made several attempts at climbing up onto the stage. 'I've got to start with me raven telling the future before I go into me knights of the

70

round table,' she explained, testing her wing span and sprinkling loose feathers everywhere.

Just in time to return some sanity to the tent, Poppa appeared to help with the stage set-up and soundcheck. He was no stranger to roadie duties and had assisted Hettie during her music days as driver, gofer and sound engineer. 'Blimey, it's a hot one out there,' he said, wiping the sweat from his brow with his paw. 'Nice to have a bit of shade in here. What needs doing?'

Muddy pointed one of her wings towards the round table. 'I'll need that up here on the stage and that screen for me quick changes. I've got to go from raven to King Arthur before I work me way through all the knights, then Merlin's the big bit at the end with the dry ice and pyros.'

Tilly was fascinated and couldn't resist asking the folk rock star a question. 'Will you be including Guinevere in your performance, Miss Fryer?'

Muddy looked up as Hettie and Poppa struggled with the table. 'I've had to edit her out. Going from chain mail to a long frock is a bit of a big ask, so I just have to pretend she's under the table. You won't miss her once I get going.'

As Muddy sorted through her props, Poppa checked her vocal mic and plugged in the small electric ukulele on which Muddy accompanied herself. Hettie and Tilly bagged two seats on the front row and sat spellbound as the musician took flight with the first song in her Arthurian cycle. Satisfied that the sound was good, Muddy clambered off the stage, placing herself out of sight of the audience which was now on its way to hear her.

If it hadn't been for Downton Tabby, Muddy Fryer's performance would have undoubtedly been the highlight of the festival. Her voice soared, her costumes enthralled, and the pyrotechnic display at the end was a master stroke, in spite of singeing a little fur here and there. Hettie was so charmed by the spectacle that she had quite forgotten that she was next up, sharing the stage with the cat whom everyone wanted to catch sight of. Reality struck when the applause eventually died down and Poppa leapt onto the stage to shove the round table to one side, quickly replacing it with two comfy armchairs which gave the stage an instant 'in conversation' look.

Hettie rose from her seat and made her way to the backstage area as Bugs Anderton took her place next to Tilly on the front row, having safely delivered her charge. The marquee had been full for Muddy's performance but now it was bursting at the seams as more and more cats squeezed themselves into the smallest of spaces to get a glimpse of the main event. She found Downton Tabby in deep conversation with all three Brontë sisters at the backstage entrance. He seemed to be waving his cane in the air as if swatting them like flies. All three sisters looked thunderous, and Hettie moved in swiftly to avert another altercation. 'Sir Downton, if you would like to follow me, I will introduce you.'

Downton Tabby looked pleased to be rescued from the resident banshees and followed Hettie into the backstage area. The Brontës headed for the hospitality tent, which had been abandoned by all but Delirium Treemints. With the exception of those four cats, the entire festival population was crammed into the events marquee for the headliner's first appearance of the weekend. Hettie had hardly finished her introduction before a deafening roar visibly lifted the roof and Downton Tabby stepped out into the limelight to a standing ovation which continued for some time. Prunella Snap raised her camera in the air in the hope of gaining the front page of the *Sunday Snout*, clicking away continuously until her film ran out and she was reduced to scrabbling around in the crush, trying to reload her camera.

Hettie proffered one of the armchairs and placed herself in the other, and the two cats sat opposite each other waiting for the applause to die down. Hettie's mind was racing. Where would she start the conversation? It wasn't just about the cat in front of her; it was about her own ability to discuss his work and entertain the hundreds of cats who now looked on in expectation. She looked for Tilly on the front row and found her squashed up with the rest of their friends – Jessie, Poppa and Bruiser, all rooting for her; Tilly raised her paw in encouragement. There was a deathly hush as the audience waited for Hettie to begin. 'Sir Downton,' she ventured. 'What first inspired you to write your TV series *In the Kitchen and Up The Stairs*?'

Hettie couldn't have asked for a better response. Downton Tabby obliged her by instantly transporting himself and the audience back to his privileged beginnings. 'I was born into a life of luxury,' he said. 'My ancestors had been granted house and lands from Tudor kings, and when my father died all those lands passed to me. I am what you may call "very rich indeed", and I thought it would be jolly good fun to give less fortunate cats a peep at what life is like when you have lots of money and lots of servants. When I was a kitten, I spent a lot of my time in the kitchen below stairs with our cook, Bessie Grump. Bessie was kind to me and gave me an insight into what it was like to be poor. We didn't pay Bessie very much, as she did get her meals and lodgings free. It was fun to see how poor our servants were and I started to write little stories about them. The poorer they were, the better my stories became. When Bessie became too old to work, we turned her out and found her a nice place at the local workhouse, where she finished her days scrubbing floors. My father enjoyed beating his servants and I would hide behind the blankets in the tack room and watch them being whipped or struck repeatedly with his riding crop. They were happy days, and I never forgot them. I wrote it all down, and when a friend of mine in publishing suggested I write a book or two, all those wonderful memories came flooding back. I added a few more bits and pieces to my original stories and – hey presto – before I knew it, I was turning the books into screenplays for television and making lots more money.'

Hettie could hardly believe what she was hearing. The inhumanity of the reply to her question had struck her dumb, but she had to continue. 'Are you pleased with the way your stories are portrayed on television?'

'Well that, my dear, is a very good question. I was a little disappointed at how much of the violence had been removed from my original screenplay – they said it wasn't suitable for eight o'clock on a Sunday evening, when kittens were getting ready for bed. But they did double their offer for the second series and allowed a wonderful scene where the lady of the house had the under-butler's paw cut off for stealing a piece of cheese. That was an excellent episode – one of my favourites actually, and almost a true story.'

'Why do you say "almost"?' picked up Hettie.

'Well, the lady in question was my great aunt Clarissa, who used to stay with us each winter. She was a game old gal, loved shooting anything that moved, a real country cat. One day, she caught the under-butler nibbling on a piece of cheese that had fallen out of her sandwich at luncheon, so she took up the cook's meat cleaver and chopped both his paws off for stealing. It was a sight to behold, and it took years for the bloodstains to fade from the grand dining-room ceiling. The TV cats thought two paws were a little over the top, so I had to settle for just the one which I thought was a shame.'

Trying to move away from the more gratuitous violence, Hettie continued. 'One of the most shocking scenes in the recent series concerned the servant who dropped dead in front of the fireplace. Was that a true story?'

Downton Tabby beamed at the audience. 'That's a super story and I witnessed it from behind a curtain in my mother's day parlour. I can't remember the cat's name now, but she was one of our many tweenies. She'd been sneezing all over the place for days – cat flu or something similar. Anyway, she was up at five laying all the upstairs fires one morning and keeled over in front of the grate in Mama's parlour. I'd been watching her for some time, pretty little thing, hardly more than a kitten. Our housekeeper turned up to check her work and found her lying dead. The shocking thing was that Mama was due any moment, as she always wrote her letters in that room each morning after breakfast. Drastic measures were taken to delay her progress by sending up an extra cup of hot chocolate and cream to her bedroom while the gardener cleared the tweenie away. He took her out in his wheelbarrow and kept her in the greenhouse while he put together a rough box to put her in. The thing was, we couldn't have Mama coming down to an untidy parlour – and having a dead servant in one's grate is *jolly* untidy.'

Hettie felt that the interview was becoming a blood sport of its own and decided to throw the event open to the paying audience. 'Would anyone like to ask a question?'

Paws shot up all over the marquee and Hettie chose a long-haired black-and-white cat at random. 'Sir Downton, have you been asked to turn other books into screenplays?'

Downton smiled down at his audience and addressed his answer in the direction of the questioner. 'Yes, I'm afraid I get sent books all the time in the hope that I'll work my magic on them. I have recently been considering writing a screenplay for Miss Brontë's *Withering Sights* but the novel requires too much work and I wouldn't want to put my name to anything below par.'

'What about doing *Jane Hair*?' came a muffled voice from the centre of the crowd, sporting a distinct Porkshire accent.

Downton Tabby smiled out at the audience in the direction of the heckler before delivering another fatal blow to the Brontës' literary talents. 'I'm no great believer in finishing other cats' work. I have never doubted the brilliance of the old Brontës, who were of their time, but the hijacking of unfinished manuscripts is piracy of the very worst kind. My advice to the Misses Brontë is to write their own books rather than lean on their ancestors. Having said that, Miss Emmeline writes very fine poetry and should be encouraged in that direction.'

'You don't mind using your own ancestors to make money, do you?' came the indignant reply from the heckler.

Another paw went up and Hettie responded immediately, wishing to head off any further trouble from the sisters who had somehow managed to force themselves into the middle of the audience. 'Yes – the cat in the string vest. What is your question?'

'Whose books would you like to adapt for TV?'

'Well, mostly mine, of course, although I do have a certain fondness for the work of P. D. Hodge – and Miss Upstart can engage with a plot, but both would have to beef up the violence for my taste.'

Polly Hodge and Nicolette exchanged looks, both clearly wanting to wipe the smile from Downton Tabby's smug face, but the audience was lapping up his pompous outbursts. And so it went on, until the hour was up. The standing ovation lasted for a full five minutes and Poppa and Bruiser cleared away the armchairs and started to move Turner Page's drum kit onto the stage to set up Furcross Convention's back line of amplifiers. The festival band would finish the Friday evening with a lively set of jigs and reels, guaranteed to send the audience home with a spring in their step. It would, however, be some time before Hettie and Tilly would see their room behind the Butters' bakery. They were in for a very long night.

CHAPTER SIX

The descending darkness had done very little to cool the temperatures of the long, hot summer's day, or to calm the additional heat created by the Brontë sisters. The audience that had gathered to see Downton Tabby made its way out of the marquee to take in the night air and sample some of the supper snacks before returning to enjoy the final entertainment of the festival's first day.

Back on stage, as Turner Page took charge of his drum kit, Hettie noticed that he had regained full use of his vocal chords and was chatting amiably with his fellow band members. Now that her public ordeal with Downton Tabby was over, she was willing to accept that Turner's nerves had got the better of him and decided to say no more about it – provided that he didn't rope her into any further Q and A's across the weekend. Downton Tabby had made a swift exit from the stage as his applause died down and Bugs Anderton – crushed in the mass exodus from the marquee – was wrong-footed in her attempt to reconnect with him. By the time she had fought her way to the backstage area, he was gone. Feeling a little rejected, she decided to make her way to the accommodation block, hoping to take him up on his earlier invitation of a small nightcap.

Bruiser and Poppa busied themselves in putting the finishing touches to Furcross Convention's set-up and helping Muddy Fryer to pack down her props; the next festival beckoned, and she was keen to get on the road. The air in the marquee was suddenly filled with the unmistakable aroma of Elsie Haddock's fish and chips as the crowds began to drift back into the tent with their suppers, and Tilly had to push through the crush to get backstage.

'You were fantastic,' she said, finding Hettie slumped behind a PA speaker.

'No thanks to the bloody Brontës! I thought I was going to have a riot on my paws for a minute. Thank God that cat in the string vest defused the situation before Charlene and co. pitched in any further.'

Tilly nodded sagely. 'Downton Tabby doesn't come across as being very nice, and he seemed to enjoy having a go at all the other authors. I don't think Nicolette or Polly are very keen on him either, but the crowd loved him.'

'Yes,' agreed Hettie. 'A little bit of notoriety goes a long way, but it makes enemies – that's the trouble.'

'Shall we have our supper here or take it home?' asked Tilly, deciding that a change of subject would do them both good. 'Those fish and chips smell lovely and the queue's probably dying down a bit by now.'

Hettie cheered up immediately at the prospect of a hot supper from the paws of Elsie Haddock, and she and Tilly made their way out of the marquee as the band launched into an energetic set of jigs and reels. By the time they reached Elsie's van, most festivalgoers had returned to the marquee to enjoy the music and the stalls that had been so busy throughout the day were closed up. The occasional cat lurched across their path, having enjoyed a little too much festival ale, but generally Hettie had to admit the clientele had been fairly passive and well behaved.

As they waited for their fish to fry, Hettie looked back towards the marquee. The distant music and the brightly lit tent gave the gardens of Furcross House an almost magical appearance, and the giant marquee glowed in the surrounding darkness.

'I think we'd better stay to the end and eat our supper here,' said Hettie, as Elsie Haddock slapped two sizzling fish on a mountain of chips. 'It's very dark outside and there could be trouble when everyone tries to leave at the same time. The festival ale seems a bit too popular and the catnip pipes are being loaded as we speak.'

Tilly giggled. 'I wonder what the Brontës would be like after a pipe or two of catnip? Do you think it would calm them down?'

Hettie choked on a chip at the very thought of it as they made their way back to the marquee, just in time to see Muddy Fryer performing an Irish step dance on stage at the invitation of the band and to the delight of the audience. 'If she doesn't get on the road soon, you'll have to find her some accommodation!' Hettie called to Tilly above the crowd.

'Perhaps she'd like to share with Ann Brontë!' Both cats joined in the foot stamping as Muddy leapt off the stage and began to dance through the audience. Even Mr Pushkin had left his desk in the library to stand by the stage, and was clapping in time to Turner's driving beat.

Muddy finally managed to dance her way to the back of the marquee, where the festival ale was being dispensed. She was rewarded with a large pint, which she downed in one before returning to the stage to hiccup her way through her big hit, 'All Around My Cat', accompanied by a loud and enthusiastic crowd. Exhausted, she collapsed at the side of the stage as

Furcross Convention pounded out a set of Scottish reels, culminating in a drum solo which any sober audience might have thought a little too long.

When the last note had been struck, the audience left the marquee fuelled by catnip and ale, and set out unsteadily for home. Hettie and Tilly watched as the trail of happy cats exited through the side entrance of Furcross House and out into Sheba Gardens, some still singing, others doing their best to walk in a straight line once the night air had claimed them.

'Well, in spite of the festival ale, that was a fairly orderly departure,' said Hettie. 'Let's go and give Bruiser and Poppa a hand with de-rigging the stage. We'll get home much quicker if we help.'

The two friends headed back towards the marquee, looking up at the night sky. It was as clear as crystal; the stars twinkled, and the moon rose to bathe everything in a ghostly blue light. The first dew had fallen on the grass and Tilly was so transfixed by her appraisal of the heavens that she slipped and fell flat on her face. 'Steady on,' said Hettie, coming to the rescue. 'That's just plain careless.'

'I didn't do it on purpose,' Tilly protested as Hettie helped her up.

'I didn't mean that *you* were careless. Look – you've tripped over a bit of canvas from Nicolette Upst . . .' Hettie froze before she could finish her sentence. The two cats stared in horror as the moon cast its light on Nicolette Upstart's pop-up merchandise stall. The stall was in its collapsed state, but sticking out from underneath its striped canvas folds was a pair of black-and-white spats. Unmistakably, the shoes belonged to Downton Tabby. Hettie moved closer and quickly realised that the whole immediate area was saturated in a sticky pool of congealed blood. 'Go and find Bruiser,' she hissed at Tilly. 'And don't say anything to anyone else. We need to see what's happened here before the jungle drums start.'

Tilly made her way to the marquee and Hettie stood as if rooted to the spot, trying to come to terms with what was in front of her. By the time Tilly returned with Bruiser, she'd convinced herself that it was all a big joke and that Downton Tabby's shoes had been placed in a pool of Elsie Haddock's best home-made tomato sauce. 'We need to move this pop-up thing to see what's going on underneath it,' she said. Bruiser took hold of the canvas structure and gave it a good tug. The torso it revealed was dressed in a bright checked suit but appeared to be missing a head. Refusing to react to the horror that had presented itself, Hettie skirted the scene looking for the missing body part, knowing instantly that the bits she already had to work with belonged to Downton Tabby.

Tilly's fish and chips rose in her throat and Bruiser stood back to gather himself, biting the back of his paw as if that would give him strength. Hettie glanced across at them and knew instinctively that they should keep busy. There was no time to lose. The murderer could be anywhere in the grounds or already wending a merry way home via Sheba Gardens. 'We need to get this covered up!' Hettie ordered, attempting to mobilise her troops. Tilly responded by whipping one of the dust sheets off the Green Peas stall and throwing it over the corpse. Things improved greatly now that they could no longer see the body, and it gave Hettie time to gather her thoughts.

'I'll go and break the news to Turner Page. Bruiser, I want you to make sure no one else leaves tonight, and I want to know who is still in the grounds. Tell them to gather in the hospitality tent. Make up any reason you like, but don't give the slightest indication of what's happened here. Tilly, I need you to go and get Bugs Anderton and all three of the Brontës, and see if you can find Downton Tabby's driver, too. Send them all to the hospitality tent. No one is to leave until I say so.'

Tilly marvelled at Hettie's rallying spirit and headed off towards the accommodation block. Bruiser followed Hettie into the marquee, where Turner Page was still packing up his drum kit, ably assisted by Mr Pushkin. As Bruiser continued on through the tent and out the other side, Hettie noticed that Muddy Fryer was sobbing at the side of the stage, while Poppa did his best to console her. Distracted from her mission, Hettie crossed over to see if the tears had any bearing on her gruesome discovery, and Muddy's sobs grew even louder as she approached. 'Whatever's the matter?' she asked.

'Someone's nicked her Excalibur,' said Poppa. 'She says it's quite valuable and she can't leave without it.'

Hettie stared at the sobbing cat. 'Well, she's right there. No one's going anywhere at the moment.'

She pulled Poppa to one side and briefly explained that she was currently searching for Downton Tabby's head, which may well have become detached from his body by Muddy Fryer's broadsword. Naturally, Poppa thought that she was joking and began to laugh until he caught sight of her expression.

'Blimey! That's a bit of a bugger,' he said. 'What can I do to help?'

'You could stand guard over the situation until I've got everyone gathered in the hospitality tent. It's just outside the marquee on the left.'

'Right-o.' Ever helpful, Poppa moved off towards the exit. Hettie coaxed Muddy off the stage and pointed her in the direction of the hospitality tent, watching as she sobbed her way across the memorial garden. Unable to put the task off any longer, she turned to the festival director, obliged to put a real damper on his first foray into the literary world of weekend gatherings. The news that Downton Tabby had been beheaded was never going to make for an easy discussion, so, to save time, she decided on the direct, no-nonsense approach, leaving Mr Pushkin to deal with the fallout and deliver his friend to the refreshment area. Then she returned to the body and, with Poppa's help, scoured the area for clues, in particular Downton Tabby's head and Muddy Fryer's broadsword.

At the same time Tilly made her way across to the accommodation block, which appeared to be in darkness. There was no sign of Bugs Anderton or Downton Tabby's driver. She let herself into the corridor and knocked on the doors allotted to the festival star; there was no response, so she moved further down the hallway and tried Charlene and Emmeline's room. All was quiet, and she knocked again. This time, a faint rustling came from within, followed by the sound of a key in the lock. The door opened to reveal Emmeline, dressed in a full-length nightdress and still wearing her festival lanyard.

'Oh, Miss Emmeline, I'm so sorry to bother you but I wondered if you and your sisters would care to join us? We're having a special presentation in the hospitality tent and it wouldn't be the same without you.'

Tilly was pleased with her fib, and it was obviously

credible because Emmeline responded favourably. 'I shall be delighted to attend, but I cannot speak for my sisters. I haven't seen them since the music began, and as I have driven all the way from Porkshire today, I decided to have an early night in preparation for my event tomorrow. However, I find that I cannot sleep without the sweet smell of the moor permeating through my window, so I will be glad to join you. If you would care to wait, I will throw on a shawl and my away-from-home slippers.' With that, Emmeline shut the door in Tilly's face and emerged five minutes later, looking every bit like one of the characters from *Withering Sights*.

The hospitality tent was buzzing with cats, all expecting an additional bonus event after what had already been a very successful day. Delirium Treemints, who had been preparing to go home, had fired up her samovar again and was busy serving teas. The day's leftover cakes and pies were piled up on a central table for the cats to pick at, and a fresh batch of festival doughnuts had magically appeared as the assembled company chatted and waited for something to happen. The mood changed on the arrival of Turner Page and Mr Pushkin, who were clearly distressed and kept themselves apart from the rest of the gathering.

Having delivered Emmeline and established that

the other two sisters were not in the tent, Tilly went off in search of them. As she rounded the corner by the accommodation block, Bugs Anderton and Downton Tabby's chauffeur emerged from the Rolls-Royce, both giggling and looking the worse for drink.

'Ah, Miss Anderton – Hettie would like everyone to go to the hospitality tent. She has a very important message to pass on.'

Bugs, a little unsteady on her legs, was propped up by the chauffeur, who also seemed to be having difficulty walking in a straight line. There was no time for Tilly to consider what had been going on in the Rolls-Royce, and at this point she didn't care. She left them to make their way to the refreshment area and retraced her footsteps back to the marquee, looking for Charlene and Ann Brontë.

Hettie and Poppa, now joined by Bruiser, were scouring the shrubbery in the moonlight, searching for the missing head. Tilly appeared from the other side of the marquee to report that all cats on-site were now gathered in the hospitality tent awaiting further developments; only the two Brontë sisters were still unaccounted for.

'Well that's the most significant bit of news we've had so far,' said Hettie, struggling out of a dense stretch of privet. 'Charlene Brontë has to be the number one suspect at the moment – she's done nothing but cause trouble since she got here. And Ann's the quiet, deadly type. I can easily see them wielding a broadsword together. Is their camper van still in the car park?' Tilly nodded. 'Well, let's have a closer look at it on our way back.'

Hettie strode purposefully towards the accommodation block, her disciples following on behind. The camper van hadn't moved from the place where Poppa had parked it. It was locked, but the window on the passenger side was wound down. Poppa reached inside and flicked the lock to open the door. Hettie peered inside, noting a picnic flask and a number of sandwich wrappers scattered about the cab. There was a half-eaten Pontefract cake stuck to the driver's seat, but no sign of a broadsword or a severed head. Behind the seats was a bright orange curtain which separated the cab from the camper. Hauling herself up into the cab, Hettie pulled the curtain to one side to reveal three neat bunk beds, one of which was folded against the wall to allow room for a small cooker and sink. 'They've got all the mod cons in here,' she said, as Tilly joined her for a look round.

'Ooh, this is lovely! If we had one of these, we could spend weeks at the seaside whenever we wanted to.' Tilly climbed onto the top bunk to see how comfortable it was, appreciating the mountain of cushions that wrapped itself around her. Looking across at the folded up bunk, she brought her favourite appraisal of the camper to an abrupt end with a cry which must have been heard in Sheba Gardens. Bruiser and Poppa responded instantly by piling into the van, and all four cats stared in disbelief at the paw sticking out from the bed.

Poppa and Bruiser untied the leather straps, holding the bunk in position, then gently let it down. The dead cat was squashed almost beyond recognition. Its mouth gaped wide in a silent scream; its body was flattened as if it had been locked in a vice. Hettie moved to get a better view of the corpse.

'Well, that's one of the missing Brontës accounted for,' she said, peering at the dead cat's chest. 'Look – her lanyard's been squashed into her skin.'

'Poor Ann,' said Tilly. 'She didn't even get to do her event. Still, she *was* quite nasty about Emmeline's poems.'

'Are you putting that forward as a motive for murder?' asked Hettie, taking a closer look at Ann Brontë's squashed face.

'Not really. I was just thinking out loud. I wonder where Charlene has got to? If we find her, we'll have the complete set.'

All four friends laughed to defuse the situation. The only cat who didn't appreciate the comment was Ann Brontë; for her, things had become a little flat.

'Come on,' said Hettie. 'Let's put this bunk back the way we found it for now. It won't do her any harm to stay here a bit longer. We'd better get over to the hospitality area – maybe Charlene has turned up there, or maybe she's hitching back to Porkshire with Downton Tabby's head in her duffle bag.'

CHAPTER SEVEN

The tent was buzzing with conversation by the time Hettie and Tilly arrived, having despatched Bruiser and Poppa to continue the search for Muddy Fryer's sword and Downton Tabby's head. Hettie entered first and noticed that the cats were gathered in clutches: Polly Hodge and Nicolette Upstart were in deep conversation with Muddy Fryer; Bugs Anderton was enjoying a festival doughnut with Downton Tabby's chauffeur; Delirium Treemints stood behind her refreshments table, sharing the occasional word with Cherry and Hilary Fudge, who both stood to attention as if their first-aid skills would be required at any moment.

Emmeline Brontë floated like a ghost from one table

to another, her long nightdress and slippers suggesting that she was in the throes of a sleepwalking episode. There was no sign of Charlene, and her absence was more than a little significant.

Hettie made her way over to the table where Turner Page and Mr Pushkin were sitting. 'I think we'd better break the news and get this over with,' she said, as Tilly joined them with two cups of tea. 'There's been another body since we last spoke. I'm afraid you're now two authors down.'

Turner Page looked ashen and Mr Pushkin gave him a hug in a rare public display of affection. Hettie continued with the facts, thinking it only fair to inform the festival's director before sharing the news with the assembled company. 'I'm afraid Miss Ann Brontë has also been murdered. She's been squashed flat in her own camper van, and it's clear that it was no accident. Charlene Brontë is nowhere to be found, which makes her my prime suspect.'

Turner Page took his head in his paws, as if trying to shut out the world. The rest of the tent fell silent and all eyes turned to Hettie, who swallowed a large gulp of tea and stood to address them. 'There's no easy way of breaking this news. Two murders have been committed here tonight, and in my capacity as head of festival security, I have called you all together to try to establish what has happened and who is responsible.'

Shock ran around the hospitality tent like a Mexican wave. Hettie took in the sea of faces, hoping to spot a reaction which was out of place, but all the cats remained frozen as they waited for her to continue. 'I apologise for keeping you all so late, but in order to eliminate each of you from our enquiries, Miss Tilly Jenkins and I will now conduct a series of interviews to establish the whereabouts of everyone at the time of the deaths.'

There was much murmuring, but it was Polly Hodge who spoke first. 'Miss Bagshot, might I ask who the victims are? I note as I look round that there are several authors missing, notably Sir Downton Tabby. You are surely not suggesting that he has fallen foul of an assassin?'

'I'm afraid that is the case, but I would prefer to discuss the details on an individual basis rather than making this an open forum.'

Polly Hodge nodded sagely, realising that Hettie didn't wish to display all her cards at once. The author's skill with murderous plots had taught her that deception and prevarication were at the heart of a detective's work, and she seemed convinced now that Hettie had everything under control.

As with many things, appearances are often misleading. In fact, Hettie had no real idea why she was there at all. Half of her felt that she should be on the trail of Charlene Brontë, who had clearly absconded, and the other half wanted to be at home, tucking into a bag of leftover festival pies. It wasn't to be, of course: she had laid out her stall and now she had to follow it through. Charlene might be the obvious suspect, but everyone gathered in the refreshment tent had the opportunity – and some a half-decent motive – for murder, and it was up to her to sort through the possibilities as quickly as she could.

'I suggest we take a table in the authors' area and invite you one by one to give an account of your movements over the last couple of hours,' she said. 'First, I would like to talk to Miss Emmeline Brontë.'

Emmeline responded with a beaming smile, as if she'd been picked for an Academy Award, and glided over to the table that Tilly had chosen for the interrogations. Tilly took out her notepad and pencil, ready to record anything of significance as Hettie gathered her thoughts and prepared to break the news of Ann Brontë's death to her sister. The rest of the cats, fuelled by the revelation of Downton Tabby's murder, created a background noise of speculation and conjecture amongst themselves.

'Miss Brontë, I'm afraid I have some terrible news,' Hettie said, beginning her interrogation. 'Your sister Ann has been murdered.'

The smile left Emmeline's face. She lowered her head and stared at the table as if in silent prayer. Hettie waited impatiently for a further reaction, but

Emmeline only continued her detailed inspection of the tablecloth. Needing to get on, and having no time for a soft-paw approach, Hettie continued, raising her voice slightly in order to command Emmeline's full attention. 'I need to establish where you and your sisters went after you left the event tonight. You were clearly together at Sir Downton's presentation, but what did you do afterwards?'

At last, Emmeline lifted her head. Hettie could see no sign of grief or shock in her eyes; there was a faraway look which suggested that she had no connection with the here and now, but that was a characteristic unique to this particular Brontë, a state of mind which those who knew her would regard as normal. Slowly, as if selecting her words from a paintbox, she said: 'My sisters have never really included me in anything. I haven't ever cared for their company because they enjoyed making fun of me. They never understood the melancholy that has beset me since my mother's death, nor the anguish to which I have been subjected in completing *Withering Sights*, when truly I am a poet. My success is unlooked for and unwanted. If Ann has died, then there is one less tormentor in my life. And now I will answer your question. I left Charlene and Ann by the bookstall after Downton Tabby's event and went straight to my room, where I prepared for bed. I remembered that I had left my journal in the camper, so I went out to fetch it and returned to my

room, where I stayed until you knocked on my door.'
Emmeline nodded towards Tilly.

'Did you meet anyone on the way back to your room, or when you went to the camper van?'

'No one in particular, although there were plenty of cats about. I did pass the time of day with that Scottish cat when I was fetching the journal – she was looking for Downton Tabby and asked me if I'd seen him.'

'Did you notice anything strange about the camper?'

Emmeline shook her head. 'It was hot and stuffy, so I left the passenger window wound down to let some air in, but that's all.'

Hettie decided to try another line of questioning. 'You don't seem to be very sad about the death of your sister, or worried that Charlene appears to be missing. Aren't you interested in what's happened to them?'

Emmeline maintained her composure. 'We have a saying in Teethly: "What has come to pass has come to pass." I will share my thoughts with the moor on my return to Porkshire.'

Hettie felt that this was a good place to stop before Emmeline treated her to a soliloquy on her favourite subject. She was getting nowhere, and there was a tent full of cats still to talk to. Dismissing the author with a brief thank you, she called for Bugs Anderton to join them and Emmeline Brontë glided off towards the refreshment table.

To say that Bugs Anderton looked sheepish as

she settled into the seat opposite Hettie would be an understatement, and her defence of the situation began immediately, even before Hettie could summon up her first question. 'Miss Bagshot, I have done my best to execute the trust you have put in me regarding the chaperoning of Sir Downton around the festival, but he quite simply disappeared at the end of his event and now you tell us that he has been murdered and it is I who feel the full weight of responsibility. I assure you that . . .'

Hettie raised her paw to bring Bugs' diatribe to an end. 'No point in crying over spilt milk. I'm sure you've done your best, and if he chose to shed his security you can hardly be blamed for that. Tell me what you did when you discovered that Downton Tabby had disappeared.'

Relieved that Hettie bore her no malice, Bugs gave a detailed account of her movements. 'Sir Downton mentioned that he would like me to join him in his rooms for a nightcap before I went home. He said he had a particularly fine Highland malt on which he would value my opinion.' Hettie and Tilly shared a look as Bugs continued. 'I looked for him everywhere backstage, and I assumed that he had already gone back to his rooms, so I went across to the accommodation block and knocked on the door to his sitting room. It was actually Darius who answered. He'd been watching something on the television – "Gobblebox", I think it was, not that I watch anything like that of course, and . . .'

Hettie raised her paw once again. 'Darius?'

'Oh yes, I'm sorry. Mr Darius Bonnet is Sir Downton's chauffeur,' Bugs explained, looking a little flushed. 'He invited me in to wait for Sir Downton, but after about twenty minutes we decided to go and sit in the Rolls-Royce. In general conversation, Darius . . . er . . . I mean Mr Bonnet . . . happened to mention that he collected road maps, and he had some lovely ones of Scotland that he wanted to show me.' Hettie and Tilly shared another look, and this time they both stifled a snigger. Tilly bit the top of her pencil while Hettie cleared her throat, and Bugs continued. 'We left the room and made our way down the corridor.'

'Did you see anyone else in the accommodation block?'

'Not exactly, although we did hear raised voices coming from one of the other rooms. It was the Misses Brontë, I think – definitely Porkshire accents. On reflection, it must have been Ann and Charlene.'

'Why do you say that?' asked Hettie, looking interested.

'A process of elimination, really. When Darius . . . er . . . when Mr Bonnet and I reached the Rolls-Royce, we bumped into Emmeline. She was looking a little lost, dressed as she is now in her

102

nightdress, and was standing by their camper van.'

'Did you speak to her?'

Bugs thought for a moment. 'I may have said something, but Darius was keen to show me his maps and he had already opened the door for me, so I got into the car with him.'

'Did you notice anyone else around the camper while you were looking at Mr Bonnet's ... er ... maps?'

'Not really. The Rolls-Royce was facing the wall and we got straight on with the Isle of Skye.'

'In that case, perhaps you could ask Mr Bonnet to join us? You can go home if you wish, but please don't discuss the matter with anyone.'

Bugs looked a little disappointed at having been so quickly dismissed; she had questions of her own that needed answers. 'Miss Bagshot, as I am obviously not a suspect, I wonder if you are able to share the details of Sir Downton's demise with me? All I know is that he has been murdered.'

'That's all you need to know for now. And as for not being a suspect, *everyone* is a suspect at this point in time.'

Bugs Anderton looked once at the grave expression on Hettie's face and rose immediately from her chair, making her way over to Darius Bonnet. The chauffeur was a good-looking cat: his short grey-and-black fur was neatly presented and his clothes were of a good quality; his bright eyes shone in the dim light of the tent, and Tilly had problems taking her eyes off him as he sat waiting to be questioned.

'Mr Bonnet,' Hettie began. 'As I'm sure you're aware by now, Sir Downton Tabby is dead and has clearly been murdered in a vicious attack. As you're the only cat here who knows him well, perhaps you would be kind enough to fill in some details for us?'

Darius Bonnet smiled and nodded his consent. 'Fire away. I'll do anything to help. He was a good guv'nor.'

'Have you been working for him long?'

'All me life, really. You see, I was born the wrong side of the hearth rug. My ma was in service to Sir Downton's family and she fell for me by mistake. She took badly and died while I was still a kitten, so the family gave me to their old chauffeur. He brought me up and taught me all about motors, so when he got too old to work, they sent him to the workhouse and gave me his job. Then Sir Downton inherited from his father and took me on as chauffeur and personal valet.'

'What was he like to work for?'

'He treated me well, I must say. He had an eye for the girl cats, so I was always getting him out of scrapes in that way, if you know what I mean. Things got a bit hectic when he got really famous with the TV and all that, but he paid me well and I've got a nice bit tucked away for a rainy day.'

Hettie couldn't help but think that the rainy day

had turned into a monsoon, but she pushed on with the questions. 'Were you aware of anyone who might want to harm him?'

'Well, that would make for quite a long list. Wherever he went, cats were jealous. It was the money, really, and the fact that he wasn't bothered what anyone thought. Like those Brontë madams, as he always called them. They were a real nuisance – turning up at events and stirring things up, writing nasty notes and leaving them on the Roller's windscreen.'

'What did the notes say?'

'Oh, "arrogant pig", "imbecilic scribbler", stuff like that. All a bit kittenish, really.'

'And which of the sisters seemed to be the ring leader in all of this?'

'To be honest, it would be hard to say. They always turn up together in that old camper, and they're a collective bag of trouble.'

'Besides the money, was there any particular reason for their behaviour?'

'Well, they were always peddling their books and wanting him to get them on TV. He told them over and over again that they weren't good enough, but some cats never listen, do they? They seemed to think that he owed it to them to help.'

'Why do you say that?'

'Because they just didn't give up, even after he'd told them he wasn't interested in their books.'

'Did he show any interest in them in other ways?'

Darius laughed and his whole face lit up, much to the appreciation of Tilly, who dropped her pencil and had to retrieve it from under the table. 'You must be joking! He liked the girls, but even he couldn't manage three at a time. And that's the thing about the Brontës – they stick together like glue.'

Hettie was thoughtful for a moment. Everything was pointing to the Brontë sisters, with Ann lying very dead in the camper, Emmeline floating about in her nightdress, and Charlene nowhere to be found. On paper, it was an open-and-shut case. But there was something wrong, and she was missing more than a head in this particular jigsaw.

'Mr Bonnet, is there anyone else at the festival who had issues with Sir Downton?'

'Like I said, he wasn't popular because he was popular. Let me see – P. D. Hodge gave him a couple of bad reviews, and he used to say that she thought she was God's gift to literary crime. Then there's Nicolette – he got a bit over-friendly there and she didn't mince her words. He was quite taken with her for a while, but she wanted nothing to do with him. Then there's that singer – she did an open air thing for him at his country house. He took to her in that chain mail, lavished her with gifts, and even gave her a yurt in his kitchen gardens, but she upped and left after a week, taking the yurt with her.'

'Are you referring to Muddy Fryer?' asked Hettie, beginning to realise that the only cat who wasn't on the list of suspects so far was Delirium Treemints.

'Yes, that's the one. Brilliant singer, though.'

'Before we finish here, I would like you to tell me where you were this evening. I didn't notice you at Sir Downton's event.'

'No, I never go to them. Not being rude, but I've heard it all before and when he's busy I can put my feet up for a bit. Sometimes I relax in the Roller till he's finished, but tonight I thought I'd catch up on a bit of TV in the room. Bugs . . . I mean Miss Anderton . . . collected him for his event and I settled down with my paper and then put "Gobblebox" on. I like to see what they're eating – it's a good laugh. Miss Anderton turned up later looking for the guv'nor as she'd missed him backstage, so we had a drink and watched a bit of TV and then I offered to show her some of my old maps in the Roller.'

'Did you meet anyone on the way to the Rolls-Royce?'

'Two of the Brontës were having a bit of a ding-dong in their room, and it sounded like one of them was crying. We could hear that all the way down the corridor. The other one was hanging around by their camper – in her nightdress, of all things.'

'Weren't you concerned for Sir Downton?'

Darius shook his head. 'Not really. Why should I be? I just assumed that he was being swamped by his fans and would turn up eventually.' As if a bolt of lightning had struck, Darius Bonnet suddenly crumpled. 'What will I do without the guv'nor?' he sobbed. 'It's the only life I've ever known. What will happen to me now he's gone?'

Both Hettie and Tilly were taken aback by the sudden change of mood, and neither felt qualified to help with a career discussion. Hettie patted his paw and suggested that he help himself to a late supper while he waited for developments. Darius looked at her through tear-filled eyes. 'But what about the guv'nor? Where is he? I should be looking after him.'

'I'm afraid that's not possible at the moment, not until my investigations have progressed. We will be moving the bodies later tonight, but at the moment we're still gathering evidence.' Hettie could have said 'looking for the rest of Downton Tabby', but she didn't want to add to the misery that sat before her. She noted that the chauffeur showed no interest in the other victim.

Dejected and still tearful, Darius rejoined the rest of the cats and was quickly comforted by Bugs Anderton, who had decided not to go home after all. Her humdrum life had been given a spark of excitement, and returning to her small terraced house would have dampened things down considerably.

'What's next?' asked Tilly, turning to a clean page in her notebook.

'I haven't got a bloody clue, but a festival pie might help. I'm starving.' Hettie stood up. 'I'm going to get us some supper and find out if Bruiser and Poppa have turned anything up. We'll have to speak to Polly Hodge, Nicolette Upstart and Muddy Fryer next, but I think we need to give the Brontës' rooms a bit of a turn over first. Are you up to that?'

Tilly's jaw dropped. 'Me? Do a room search?'

Hettie nodded. 'Yes, you. Why not? With all those detective books you read, you should know how it goes by now.'

Tilly's chest puffed out on its own, highlighting the stains she'd collected on her T-shirt throughout the day. Not since she'd inherited Hettie's old business mac had she felt so important. In spite of her age, she had started as office junior at the No. 2 Feline Detective Agency and now, after only a few months, she was being given the opportunity to take on one of the top jobs of detection – a room search, and all the responsibility that came with it. 'What should I be looking for?' she asked.

'Anything out of place. Emmeline mentioned a journal, so it would be good to have a flick through that, and obviously you must see if there's anything relating to Downton Tabby lying around – like his head, for instance.' Tilly shrank back in horror until

109

she realised that Hettie was joking, but the thought of finding a missing body part took the edge off her excitement a little. 'Let's meet back here in half an hour,' Hettie said, standing up. 'Have you got the spare set of keys to the accommodation block?'

Tilly checked in her shoulder bag, and the two cats made their way back to the rest of the assembled company. As they appeared from the authors' dining area, a deathly hush settled over the room and Hettie responded by addressing them en masse. 'I must ask that you all remain here in the hospitality tent for a little longer,' she said. 'Due to the severity of the situation, I think it is important that you stay together whilst my operatives and I do the necessary investigations around these murders. I should warn you that it is my intention to set up a temporary mortuary in the authors' dining area, and I would appreciate it if you could steer clear of that part of the tent out of respect for the dead. Miss Delirium Treemints will, I'm sure, be happy to continue to serve hot drinks, and there's plenty of festival food to keep you happy. I think you should prepare yourselves for a long night.'

A collective murmur went up around the tent. Hettie loaded a tray with pies and festival doughnuts to keep her own troops going, and left the festivalgoers in the safe paws of Delirium, who was learning to cope with a new-found importance after being mentioned by name in Hettie's despatches. Hettie and Tilly left the tent together and went their separate ways – Tilly to the accommodation block, and Hettie to the main marquee to look for Bruiser and Poppa.

CHAPTER EIGHT

Hettie found Poppa first. He was emerging from under the stage in the marquee, his black-and-white face and whiskers covered in cobwebs. 'No luck yet,' he said, as a giant sneeze shot his sunglasses off the top of his head. He picked them up, looking pleased. 'Nice one! I was wondering where I'd put them. Good pair of shades, these. Any more bodies?'

Hettie had always admired Poppa's ease in any situation. His laid-back attitude in times of crisis had served her well during her years in the music business – and there had been plenty of crises to be laid-back about. They had remained friends, and Poppa had the uncanny knack of turning up whenever Hettie most needed him; he had the advantage of understanding her better than any other male cat she knew.

'No, no more bodies,' she said, 'but no Charlene bloody Brontë either.'

Bruiser, hearing their voices, joined them in the backstage area. 'Just started spittin' with rain out there. Do yer want us to shift the body before the downpour comes? It's really hot and muggy. I reckon we're in fer a mighty big storm any minute.'

As if on cue, the marquee was suddenly lit up by a streak of lightning and rolls of distant thunder rumbled around them. 'That's all we need,' said Hettie, as the three cats dashed out into the stalls area. 'Let's wrap the body in the sheet. It'll be easier to carry and I don't want anyone noticing that the head's missing.'

Bruiser and Poppa pulled the sheet away from Downton Tabby's body and laid it on the ground. Hettie stared down at the check-suited corpse, thinking how very ridiculous it looked without its head. It occurred to her that if Muddy Fryer's broadsword *had* been used, the murder had the feel of an execution, almost medieval in its nature. How very different from the pathetic vision of Ann Brontë's squashed pelt in the camper van. For the first time, it struck Hettie that she might be looking for two murderers, not one.

The rain had begun to fall steadily in large droplets. Bruiser took the body by the shoulders, Poppa by the feet, and they lifted it gently onto the sheet, folding the sheet over the corpse and knotting the makeshift shroud at both ends. Hettie led the way back to the refreshment tent.

'Let's take it in round the back – there's a flap in the canvas there.' Bruiser and Poppa followed her, managing to complete their task seconds before the heavens opened to subject Furcross House and its grounds to the worst summer storm in the town's memory. The rain lashed down on the tent and water rushed off the roof, creating an avalanche of gushing torrents as the lightning circled overhead, selecting points of interest to touch with its deadly fingers. The cats huddled together in the main part of the tent, where there was nothing left to do but eat pies and wait for the storm to pass.

The accommodation block was in darkness when Tilly reached it. The night air was oppressive, and she was pleased to let herself into the corridor, which was a little cooler than the temperature outside. She reached for the light switch and felt instantly better when she could see the doors that peppered the hallway. Scratching her head, she tried to remember who was staying where. The Brontës had made it clear that Emmeline and her poetry were an unwelcome combination, but who had drawn the short straw? And had they stuck to their domestic arrangements? Both the rooms allocated to the sisters would have to be searched, and they stood opposite each other. Tilly decided on the single room first and unlocked the door.

A suitcase lay on the floor, open but not unpacked, and the room was tidy. The first thing she needed to establish was whose room it was, and the stack of books on the bedside table left her in no doubt: four identical copies of *The Brontës of Teethly*, Ann's autobiography. Tilly flipped through some of the pages, turning to the black-and-white photo section in the middle of the book. There they all were, surrounded by relatives: kitten pictures; family outings; a stark and rather dramatic picture of the parsonage they all lived in; and a striking picture of an elderly cat, poised with a catapult especially for the camera.

Tilly put a copy of the book to one side to look at in more detail over a pie and a cup of tea, then turned to Ann Brontë's suitcase. She sifted carefully through the clothes, finding nothing to interest her, but a couple of newspapers at the bottom showed more promise. One of them, the *Teethly Gazette*, announced that Downton Tabby would be filming his latest TV series at Teethly Grange, a substantial house and parkland which he owned on the edge of the moor. Tilly noted that the front-page photo of the TV celebrity had been defaced and now looked more like a goat than a cat, with horns and a short, pointed beard. She could see no reason for keeping the second newspaper until she turned to the inside pages: circled in red was a review of Ann's biography, heralding it as a breath of fresh Porkshire air and comparing it favourably to both Emmeline and Charlene Brontë's efforts; the review went even further, suggesting that completing old manuscripts did not a novelist make, and that Ann Brontë was the real talent of the three authors. Looking to the bottom of the column, Tilly wasn't surprised to learn that the reviewer was Downton Tabby himself. It interested her to see that he had obviously liked Ann's book – unless, of course, he'd been playing the sisters off against each other – and, as Ann had no further need of them, Tilly added the newspapers to the book, ready to take away with her. She gave the room a final inspection, including a quick look under the bed, and found nothing more than a half-eaten pork pie which Ann had clearly discarded earlier.

Gathering up her reading material, she left the room and crossed the hallway to unlock the door opposite, but there was no need; the door wasn't locked. She paused for a moment before going inside, and a note of caution ran through her mind: what if Charlene had been in the room all the time? Emmeline had answered the door earlier, but she might have lied about Charlene's absence. Slowly, she pushed the door open wider, letting the light in from the hallway; to her relief, the room appeared to be empty, but no sooner had her heart regained its normal rhythm than a crack of thunder sent her nerves jangling. The room was filled fleetingly with an arcing streak of lightning, then all was black. Fighting to gain control, Tilly reached for the light switch but nothing happened. The corridor, too, was now in darkness. Logic should have told her that the raging storm had knocked out the electricity supply, but there is rarely room for logic when fear comes knocking.

Tilly moved forward to the window, hoping for another flash of light, and it came again, this time blinding her for several seconds. She stumbled against one of the beds, catching her foot in something dangling from it. The lightning obliged her once more, long enough to guide her to a small torch on one of the bedside tables. She lunged for it as the returning darkness engulfed her, but it rolled off the table and onto the floor. Tilly crawled after it, feeling her way across the carpet, but she froze as her paw connected with another cat's foot. She looked up as the room filled with light again, and there, staring down at her, was Charlene Brontë, her face contorted, her eyes bulging and her mouth open wide.

Instinctively, Tilly rolled away as the point of the broadsword missed her by an inch and buried itself deep into the floor. She gathered herself and made blindly for the door, crashing into the post as she fought her way back out into the corridor, then ran the length of the hallway and out into the storm without looking back.

It would be true to say that Tilly hardly noticed the rain. She stumbled and splashed her way across the memorial garden, colliding with gravestones and willing the lightning to come again and show her a path to safety. At last, the hospitality tent rose like a giant, white mother ship out of the violence of the storm, a safe refuge and an end to the terror which pursued her.

Hettie was finishing off her third festival doughnut when Tilly made her dramatic entrance into the tent. She was unrecognisable at first, a ball of wet, muddy fur which burst through the tent flap and came to an ungainly halt by Delirium Treemints' beverage table. Hilary and Cherry Fudge reacted immediately, going into their checklist of first-aid procedures, and Tilly was too traumatised to resist as they wrestled her to the ground, putting her into the recovery position and feeling for abrasions and broken bones. Eventually, she struggled free of the Florence Nightingale routine; she might well resemble something from the war-torn fields of the Crimea, but bandages and ointments would have to wait.

Hettie wiped the sugar from her whiskers and ran over to her friend, flanked by Bruiser and Poppa. The rest of the cats gathered round expectantly, and Delirium Treemints offered one of her starched white tablecloths to Tilly, who had begun to shake uncontrollably. She pulled the cloth around her,

119

grateful for its warmth, and did her best to stop her teeth from chattering.

'What happened to you?' Hettie asked, alarmed and concerned.

Staring out at the sea of faces, all waiting for a response, and expecting her attacker to burst into the tent at any moment wielding Muddy Fryer's broadsword, Tilly pulled Hettie closer and whispered: 'Charlene Brontë's gone mad! She's out there now, and she tried to kill me with the sword. She's hiding in her and Emmeline's room. I must have disturbed her. I was so frightened, I just ran and ran.'

There was no time to lose, and Hettie beckoned Bugs Anderton out of the crowd. 'Take Tilly to the authors' area and sit with her until I get back. Make sure she has a cup of hot, sweet tea, and don't let anyone bother her.'

Before she had even finished the sentence, Delirium was spooning six sugars into a cup. Tilly was helped to her feet by Bugs and steered away from prying eyes.

As Hettie, Bruiser and Poppa prepared to leave the tent, Polly Hodge spoke up. 'Miss Bagshot, would you be kind enough to explain to us what is happening?'

Hettie turned to the author, conceding that the question wasn't unreasonable. 'If I *knew* what was happening, I would be more than happy to let you know. All I can tell you is that there's a killer out there who needs to be caught.' With that, she swept out of the tent followed by Bruiser and Poppa, leaving the other cats in stunned silence. So shocked were they by her parting comment that no one noticed Emmeline Brontë slipping out of the back entrance and into the storm.

CHAPTER NINE

Regardless of her mission, Hettie was pleased to leave the tent behind; it had become hot and claustrophobic, and she welcomed the rain beating down on her face. Within minutes, all three cats were soaked to the skin. The storm was relentless, flooding the ground beneath their paws and making visibility almost impossible. They made slow progress across the memorial garden, and dark shapes loomed up before them as Poppa swept their path with his torch, a tool of the trade which always hung from his belt.

'I think we should take a look in the accommodation block,' Hettie cried before another roll of thunder swallowed the rest of her sentence. The door to the block was wide open and Poppa led the way down the corridor. Tilly's shoulder bag lay outside the rooms allocated to the Brontës, together with a book and some newspapers which she'd abandoned in her flight to safety. The door to one of the rooms was slightly ajar, and it was Bruiser who – moving Hettie to one side – kicked it open and crouched ready to spring at anything that came for him. Apparently the room was empty and Poppa went ahead, shining the torch into every corner. Hettie noticed that the floor was wet. 'Looks like our murderer gave chase to Tilly and came back here afterwards,' she said. 'I wonder why? Did anyone notice if the camper was still parked outside?'

Bruiser responded immediately by going to check, and returned seconds later. 'It's still there, next to the Roller.'

'In that case, Charlene Brontë is here somewhere and the sooner we find her, the better. According to Tilly, she's behaving like a homicidal maniac. I think we need to split up – we've got a lot of ground to cover and this storm makes everything much more difficult. Bruiser, you take the marquee and stalls area. I think the library's locked, so she won't be able to get into the main building, but, for God's sake, be careful. I'll have a look round here, and Poppa – you check out the camper and the Rolls-Royce. They're both good places to hide.'

Bruiser took off like a rocket, but Poppa lingered.

'Are you sure you'll be all right? No point in being brave when you don't have to. Why don't we check this out together?'

Resisting the urge to hug him, Hettie agreed and the two cats set about the room search that Tilly had been forced to abandon. 'This bed's seen some action,' said Poppa, shining his torch up and down its length. 'Looks like someone's been tied to it and then chewed their way out.'

Hettie stared down at the frayed bits of cord. 'Shine that torch on the bedside cabinet. Look – what's that?'

Poppa moved forward and picked up a large wad of cotton wool. 'Blimey, it's chloroform,' he said, giving it a good sniff. 'That's all a bit Victorian – what with that and the mad cat in the attic.'

'What do you mean?' asked Hettie, looking confused.

'Well, it's all a bit *Jane Hair*, isn't it? The mad cat in the attic roams about at night setting fire to everyone's bed curtains, so they have to keep her sedated and locked up. She even has a minder who chains her to the wall when she's having one of her outbursts.'

Hettie was quite taken aback by Poppa's knowledge of Charlene Brontë's novel. 'I didn't have you down as the bonnet drama type.'

'Must be all those long, wet Sundays on me houseboat. It was *Withering Sights* that got me started on the Brontës. I've had a couple of holidays on the

125

Porkshire Moors – good ale and bad weather, and that book's got it all. There's not a decent cat in the whole thing. Nasty pieces of work, the lot of them.'

It had occurred to Hettie that she was obviously at a disadvantage when it came to the Brontës. She rarely picked up a story book, preferring fact to fiction but, as Poppa had pointed out, the two were clearly entwined as far as the Porkshire sisters were concerned. The big question was who had tied whom to the bed? And, if this situation *had* been going on, why hadn't Emmeline Brontë mentioned it when she was questioned? Hettie could feel one of her headaches coming on. She needed some space to process the information which was filling her mind with possibilities; instead, she found herself in the middle of a thunderstorm with a maniac on the loose, a tent full of fidgeting cats to pacify, and a body count which threatened to rise at any minute.

Poppa shone his torch on the other bed in the room. There was an untidy pile of clothes strewn across it, and Hettie walked over to take a closer look. 'They were wearing stuff like this when they arrived,' she said. She sifted through the bundle and found a bunch of keys at the bottom of the pile. 'I suppose these must be for the camper van. They're sticky.'

The beam of the torch fell onto the keys in Hettie's paw. 'Blimey, its blood!' Poppa said. 'And look – it's all over the clothes and the bedcover.'

Hettie threw the keys back onto the bed as if they'd burnt her. 'It's like a nest of bloody vipers in here! Or perhaps a chamber of horrors would be closer to the mark. There was no visible blood on Ann Brontë, so I think we have to assume that this belongs to Downton Tabby. I imagine there was quite a fountain of it when his head left his shoulders. We need to speak to Emmeline Brontë again. I think you should fetch her and bring her here – she's the only one that can explain what's been going on in this room. She obviously knows a lot more than she's saying, and I think we should take her to visit the corpse in the camper. That might stir her memory.'

Poppa grabbed Tilly's shoulder bag, newspapers and book, then left Hettie with the torch and struck out across the memorial gardens to fetch Emmeline. His head was down against the driving rain, and the figure standing by the potting shed under the trees went unnoticed.

Hettie continued her search of the room. There were more clothes in an unruly pile on a chair, two suitcases bulging with identical outfits, and a journal on the table by the window. Hettie flicked through some of the pages. The writing looked like a spider had crawled across the paper, dragging the ink behind it. It wasn't a conventional diary of dates and appointments, but appeared to be page after page of disconnected thoughts and tiny drawings. The thoughts were probably interesting, but there was no time for Hettie to indulge herself in them: there was still the small matter of Downton Tabby's head to find, and Charlene Brontë could burst through the door at any minute, wielding Muddy's Excalibur. Hettie put the journal to one side as a job for Tilly and continued to shine the torch around the room. She swept the flashlight across the two beds again, knowing that she would have to look under them before the room search was complete. She chose the one with the bloodied clothes first and lifted the sheet, fully expecting to come face-to-face with matted fur and a disembodied stare; to her relief, there was nothing there at all. Moving swiftly to the other bed, she crouched low and shone the light underneath; again, there was nothing horrific to greet her – only a small hand torch which she picked up as Poppa came back into the room, even more soaked than when he had left.

'Bad news, I'm afraid. The bird has flown, which is a bit of a sod, and they're getting a bit uptight in the hospitality tent. Muddy Fryer is flapping about her next gig and how she can't afford to miss it, and Turner Page has gone to pieces and is crying his eyes out.'

'They're welcome to sort this bloody mess out themselves if they'd prefer,' said Hettie. 'I'm not exactly thrilled at having to deal with a headless corpse, a flat-packed author, and what now appears to be two mad sisters on the loose in the middle of a thunderstorm.'

'Good points, well made,' said Poppa, as another streak of lightning lit up the room. 'I wonder how Bruiser's getting on? He's been gone for a while.'

'Maybe we should go and see if we can find him. With two Brontës out there, we need strength in numbers. Why would Emmeline want to put herself in danger, do you think? Or is she in league with Charlene?'

Poppa shrugged his shoulders. 'Maybe we should leave them to it. With a bit of luck, they'll kill each other.'

'Don't tempt me,' Hettie said, snatching Emmeline's journal from the table and marching towards the door. 'Let's find Bruiser and sort this out once and for all. We should be able to corner them. My guess is that they'll find some shelter and lay low till morning, so we need to flush them out. I'll drop this off in the tent first and see how Tilly is.'

Hettie and Poppa, now armed with two torches, splashed their way across to the hospitality tent. The rain was still sheeting down but the thunder had become more distant, and Hettie was relieved that the worst of the storm was over. In fact, she could hardly have been more wrong: the worst part of this particular nightmare was only just beginning.

* * *

There was a reception committee waiting at the entrance to the hospitality tent. Mr Pushkin was doing his best to remain calm and speak as the voice of reason amid a sea of cats who were tired, irritable and more than a little frightened. Emmeline Brontë's departure from the tent had encouraged those left behind to think that they, too, should be heading home – or, in Muddy's case, to the next gig. And in spite of Hettie's request, Downton Tabby's headless body had been viewed out of natural inquisitiveness by all of the cats except Delirium Treemints, whose nerves required no further stimulation.

Polly Hodge stepped forward as soon as Poppa and Hettie appeared. 'Miss Bagshot, I think we have waited long enough. Do you bring news which will put our minds at rest? We would all like to go home to our beds.'

Hettie looked at the huddle of cats and had to agree that there was very little reason to detain them any longer. It was clear to her that Charlene Brontë was guilty of the murder of Downton Tabby, perhaps with help from Emmeline, but that had nothing to do with the rest of the cats – unless one of them had squashed Ann Brontë in an entirely separate incident, and that was a long shot even to Hettie's creative abilities. She raised her paw to silence the muttering.

'My job at this festival is to try to keep everyone safe,' she began, 'which is why I've asked you to

130

remain together in this tent. I'm now in a position to lay out some facts, and those of you who wish to leave afterwards can do so at your own risk. Sir Downton Tabby was viciously attacked and murdered at some point during Furcross Convention's performance. Close to this time, Ann Brontë was also murdered in her camper van. In the course of a room search, Tilly was subsequently attacked by Charlene Brontë and has had a narrow escape from Muddy Fryer's broadsword.'

Hettie's words were making an impact: even Turner Page had stopped snivelling into Mr Pushkin's handkerchief. 'We have found evidence to suggest that Charlene Brontë was at least present at the death of Downton Tabby,' she continued, 'and she seems to have been holding one of her sisters hostage in the room they shared. I believe that hostage to be Emmeline Brontë, who has foolishly left the safety of this tent. Now, there are several things I need to do to complete my investigations. It would be helpful, although not essential, to establish why Charlene Brontë has taken against certain cats, including her own sisters. While she is at large, she remains a threat to us all and so it is my intention to find her before daylight. My final quest is to reunite the head of Downton Tabby with his body.'

There was a collective intake of breath as the assembled company finally realised its good fortune in having such a capable pair of paws to lead the dangerous and macabre investigation. Satisfied that her words had hit exactly the right spot, Hettie felt comfortable enough to issue a parting shot before going to check on Tilly.

'If any of you wish to leave, then by all means do – but you're now aware that I can't be held responsible for your safety outside this tent.'

Polly Hodge stepped forward again. 'Miss Bagshot, we are most grateful to you and to your colleagues for the work you are doing to solve this nasty situation, and we thank you for bringing us up to speed. I, for one, will heed your warning and shall remain here until the Misses Brontë are apprehended.'

A general nod of agreement went round the tent, stopping only when it reached Muddy Fryer. 'What about me gig? If I don't show, I don't get paid. I should have been on the road hours ago, and what about me sword? That's the centrepiece of me Arthurian cycle. You can't have Arthur without Excalibur.'

Although she was a fan of Muddy's music, Hettie felt that the singer herself had lived a little too long in the world of folk heroes and Knights of the Round Table to grasp the full reality of the situation.

'As I've said, you *are* free to leave. I'm sure we can send the sword on to you if we can convince Charlene Brontë to part with it.'

Turner Page decided to make a rare interjection.

'Miss Fryer, please stay here where you are safe. By way of compensation, I'm happy to pay you a further performance fee to cover your next . . . er . . . gig, and we would be delighted if you would consider an impromptu performance of some of your songs while Miss Bagshot and her assistants continue their investigations.'

Hettie could have kissed the festival director, but she didn't want to offend Mr Pushkin. Muddy, now financially solvent for another day, climbed onto one of the tables as the cats gathered around. She began to sing, and Hettie recognised the first few notes of 'Long Lankin', a famous murder ballad about a serial killer. It was one of her favourites, but not entirely appropriate at this particular time. She made her way over to Tilly, listening reluctantly to the words of the song: 'There was blood all in the kitchen, there was blood all in the hall, there was blood all in the parlour, where my lady she did fall.'

Tilly looked much better. Her long tabby coat had dried out, although it would benefit from a good comb, but her *Fur in the Sunlight* T-shirt was in shreds and would certainly have to be despatched to the duster bag in the staff sideboard when they finally returned home.

'How are you?' Hettie asked, absent-mindedly helping herself to one of Betty Butter's steak and ale pies.

'Much better. I've been so worried about all of you, though. Where are Bruiser and Poppa?'

'Poppa's listening to Muddy and Bruiser's still out there. We were just going to look for him but I wanted to check you were OK first. If you're feeling up to it, you could take a look through Emmeline's journal. I found it in the room. There might be something connected to the case, but don't ask me what.' She posted the final crust of the pie into her mouth and noticed the newspapers and the copy of Ann's book which Poppa had left with Tilly. 'Anything significant in there?'

'Yes, I think there is. I found the newspapers at the bottom of Ann's suitcase when I was searching her room. Downton Tabby was going to film his next TV series in Porkshire, near where the Brontës live, and someone's defaced his picture. There's a review of Ann's book, too – it's by Downton Tabby, and he makes it plain that Charlene and Emmeline aren't his favourite authors.'

'What about Ann Brontë? Did he like her book?'

'Oh yes. He says she's the best of the lot.'

Hettie shook her head in a bewildered fashion. 'I think you'd better take a look at that biography – maybe the answer's in there. In the meantime, Poppa and I had better get back out there and find Bruiser.'

Tilly picked up Ann Brontë's biography and Hettie made her way back to the staff refreshment area.

134

Muddy was enjoying rapturous applause as Long Lankin and his accomplice were brought to justice on 'the gallows high', and, as she left the tent with Poppa, Hettie couldn't help but think that folk ballads had the edge on reality. Justice always seemed to prevail in them, no matter what.

CHAPTER TEN

Hettie was relieved to see that the storm had continued to die down, and the rain now came in sudden gusts carried on the wind rather than the deluge they had endured earlier. Bruiser had now been gone for some time, and she was worried about him. Although he was instinctively a fighting sort of cat, his days as a warrior had disappeared when he entered his middle years; the only evidence of them now were the scars on his face and an ear that was a shadow of its former self, only half the size of the other one. He'd lost a few teeth along the way, too, mostly sunk into opponents as he defended his territories, but now, as with many older cats, he'd earned his days in the sunshine – or, on winter nights, curled up by the paraffin stove in his shed at the bottom of the Butter sisters' garden.

'Let's check out the marquee first,' Hettie suggested to Poppa. 'He's probably sheltering in there.'

They picked their way through pools of water, shining their torches on the devastation wrought by the storm. The festival bunting lay in strings across the muddy ground, or hung disconnected in the shrubbery; there was rubbish everywhere – empty paper cups and plates strewn across the grass, and plastic carrier bags caught in the trees. The summer flowers that Mr Pushkin had nurtured throughout the spring bowed their heads low to the ground, tears of rain dripping from their petals onto the sodden earth. In the distance, the town's clock chimed three, reminding Hettie that it would be some time before the first glimpse of dawn, a much-needed return of light after this night of horror. It was still warm, and in some places a fine mist rose from the ground. Conscious of the danger that lurked unseen in the grounds of Furcross House, the two cats stuck together, taking it in turns to watch their backs and looking out for the slightest movement, aware that Charlene Brontë could strike at any moment.

All was peaceful in the marquee. It had stood up to the storm and the expanse of grass it covered was dry underfoot. A couple of battery lanterns still swung from the festival bar at the back of the tent, and Poppa was quick to collect them for some extra light.

Hettie sat on the edge of the stage, staring out at the sea of empty chairs. 'I wonder what will happen in the morning?' she said, turning to the running order which was stuck to the side of the tent. 'There'll be hundreds of cats descending on Furcross, all expecting another fun day of books and music. The whole thing was due to kick off at ten with Emmeline Brontë's main event, followed by a panel with Polly Hodge and Nicolette Upstart – whatever that is. Then it's a dulcimer workshop and lunch, and – wait for it – two bloody hours of Downton Tabby, all rounded off by afternoon tea with Ann Brontë and her biography.'

Poppa joined Hettie on the stage. 'Well, looking on the bright side, the book sales will be up as soon as the news breaks. We could turn it all into a waxwork show and stick the bodies up on stage in room settings for the punters to photograph. Pity about the missing head, though.'

'Yes, and Ann Brontë would look a little too thin.'

The two friends laughed out loud as another crack of thunder rolled across the sky above them, heralding the return of the storm. Minutes later, the rain was bucketing down in a deafening assault on the roof of the marquee.

'I reckon this rain will drive Bruiser back in here,'

said Poppa, watching the water gush off the roof through the open flap of the marquee. 'We'll be drowned if we go out now. Maybe he's legged it back to refreshments or the accommodation block.'

Hettie rarely disagreed with Poppa, but this time she had a terrible feeling that Bruiser was in grave danger, perhaps even lying mortally wounded somewhere; it wasn't like him to disappear when a job needed doing. 'I think we should carry on searching for him. He might be sheltering in the stalls area.'

Poppa nodded and passed one of the lanterns to Hettie. The two cats left the safety of the marquee just in time to see the ghostly figure of Emmeline Brontë screeching past them in her sodden nightdress, heading in the direction of the memorial gardens. The brief glimpse that Hettie caught of her showed an expression of sheer terror, with bulging eyes and lips pulled back in an insane grimace as if the devil himself were giving chase.

Poppa and Hettie waited to see if her pursuer would appear, but nothing showed itself. 'Come on!' cried Hettie as a bolt of lightning hit the ground in front of them, scorching the grass. Poppa pushed ahead, attempting to shield her from the driving rain which now blinded them. The storm's ferocity showed no sign of abating, and the pools of standing water grew into lakes before them. In the memorial gardens, they could only stand in helpless horror at the sight that met them; like some ancient, vile banshee, Charlene Brontë stood bracing herself against the full force of the storm, the broadsword raised above her head, her victim bleeding at her feet.

Afterwards, every time Hettie recalled the scene in her mind, it played out in a jerky slow motion: the raised sword; Charlene Brontë's distorted face as saliva dripped from her fangs; the death-curdling screech that came from somewhere deep inside her as she slowly brought the sword down onto Bruiser's crouched and bleeding body. The lightning was swift and accurate, given the conductor it was looking for by the point of the sword. In a spray of sizzling sparks, it shot through the steel into Charlene's body, and Hettie would never forget the intense smell of burning flesh. Charlene Brontë stood like a blackened effigy burnt into the landscape, her charred skin welded to her skeleton, her eye sockets empty, and the broadsword still in her paws.

Poppa was the first to react, springing forward to where Bruiser lay, but there was so much blood that it was hard to tell if he was dead or alive. Hettie finally pulled herself together. There was a wheelbarrow parked by the potting shed to her left and she splashed across to it, wheeling it back to where Bruiser lay and doing her best to ignore the imposing figure of a rather overcooked Brontë sister which seemed to dominate the skyline. Together, she and Poppa gently lifted Bruiser into the wheelbarrow.

'Can I help?' The voice came from behind them, and Hettie turned to see Emmeline Brontë looking like she had just emerged from the town's boating lake. Her nightdress clung to her, splattered with mud, and her eyes were full of tears; she looked lost and utterly alone. Her festival name tag – smudged and almost unreadable – hung round her neck like some incongruous foreign body, the only tangible link with reality. Whatever the issues that existed between her and her sister, she had witnessed the worst death imaginable, a vision that no amount of time would eradicate.

Poppa took up the wheelbarrow and Hettie steered Emmeline away from what remained of her sister. The bedraggled company made quite an impressive entrance when it finally reached the hospitality tent, but the jubilant welcome was soon silenced by the serious nature of Bruiser's condition. Hilary and Cherry Fudge had made themselves comfortable under Delirium Treemints' beverage table and had to be roused from their slumbers. Immediately, they sprang into action. While Poppa and Hettie lifted Bruiser out of the wheelbarrow and laid him on one of the authors' tables, Cherry called for hot water and Delirium obliged from her samovar. Tilly helped Hilary to rip up a tablecloth, and they bathed the wounds which were now visible and still bleeding. Bruiser lay still and lifeless, his fur matted around the cuts. The worst of the injuries had cut deeply into his shoulder, presenting a gaping hole.

Hilary grabbed her first-aid manual and quickly turned to the chapter on wounds. 'According to this, we have to pack the hole with something and put a pad on it to stop the bleeding,' she said.

Cherry responded by pulling out a padded dressing which she'd prepared earlier. Feeling completely helpless, Tilly grabbed one of Bruiser's paws and squeezed it as the first-aiders worked on his injuries. The rest of the tent had been stunned into silence. Bugs Anderton helped the traumatised Emmeline Brontë to a chair, giving Delirium Treemints a nod on the way. A cup of tea full of sugar was delivered at once, together with the last of the clean tablecloths to wrap around Emmeline's shoulders. Hettie and Poppa – now feeling the shock waves from their ordeal – sat quietly munching on the last of the festival pies, too tired to speak but keeping a watchful eye on Bruiser for any sign of recovery.

The silence, when it came, was disconcerting: the storm which had hurled itself around them suddenly lost all its power, and the cats huddled together to discuss the latest developments lowered their voices in relief, no longer needing to shout to make themselves heard above the cacophony outside. The joyful noise of rattling tea cups as Delirium distributed another round of hot drinks with shaky paws brought sanity back to a world where fear and suspicion had dominated. Hettie looked round the tent with tired eyes, moving from one face to another. Darius Bonnet sat dejected and grief-stricken next to his master's corpse; Polly Hodge, always so confident, suddenly looked old and fragile; Muddy Fryer seemed in a state of collapse, having given up the whole of her repertoire in a home fires burning sort of way; and Nicolette Upstart's enthusiasm for life seemed to have drained away along with the contents of her tea cup, her winning smile abandoned at the starting post. And what a disappointment for Turner Page. He sat staring into space while Mr Pushkin filled his ears with words he didn't hear. All those months of planning, meetings, petitions, and fundraising, only for the excitement to end in tragedy. But why? That was the question, and now the perpetrator could no longer disrupt the natural order of things, there was time to consider her motivation.

Hettie turned her gaze on Emmeline Brontë, sitting swaddled in a tablecloth. The figure of tragedy she presented was well earned: forced into writing a book she didn't want to write, being continually wrenched from a peaceful existence where her fragile nature flourished and being deprived of the opportunity to pursue the creative art in which she excelled. Hettie couldn't help but feel that the death of her two progressively greedy sisters might be the making of her if the horror of the night's work could be channelled into something positive – and something positive was just about to happen.

'He squeezed back!' shouted Tilly from the first-aid table. 'He's coming round.'

Hettie leapt across the tent to Bruiser's side as Hilary and Cherry Fudge stood back from their patient, sharing nods of pride and satisfaction. Bruiser's head rolled from side to side as if he were checking that it was still attached to his body, then he opened his eyes to a rapturous round of applause. Even Darius Bonnet had forsaken his master to join in the celebration. 'Well, that's the last time we let you fall asleep on a job,' said Hettie, resisting the urge to dance a jig round the tent.

Bruiser smiled, then suddenly winced as the pain in his shoulder reminded him of his injuries. 'Where is she? You gotta stop 'er before she gets all of us.'

Hettie moved closer. 'Don't worry, it's all over. She won't be bothering anyone ever again. You just have to get better – that's all that matters now.'

Bruiser struggled to sit up, and Cherry Fudge

placed her first-aid bag behind his head as the first signs of daylight entered through the tent flap, followed by a commotion fit for the slapstick sequence in any good pantomime. Betty Butter was first over the threshold, clad in wellingtons and a Pacamac and balancing a tray of fresh eggs on top of a giant pack of bacon. She was instantly followed by Beryl, whose face was obscured by a mountain of freshly baked bloomers.

'Whatever's been going on?' Betty demanded, depositing her load onto the counter by the temporary field kitchen. 'My sister and I have been worried sick, haven't we?'

Beryl relieved herself of the bread and nodded earnestly as Betty continued. 'We thought we'd get the breakfasts set up before the staff arrived on account of the storm, but when we went to wake Mr Bruiser his bed hadn't been slept in and there was no sign of Miss Scarlet in her shed. Then we checked on Hettie and Miss Tilly, and there was no sign of them either. We had to call Tiddles' Taxis to bring us in. He was none too pleased at getting up early, I can tell you, especially with the streets running with floodwater.'

Betty and Beryl busied themselves unpacking the breakfast items and set two large frying pans on the makeshift stove. 'We've had to leave the sausages and the black pudding by the library,' Beryl said, taking up where her sister had left off. 'We couldn't manage to carry any more, and we're up to here in mud as it is.' She glanced down at her wellingtons for effect, giving Betty the opportunity to pick up the conversation.

'I'll never quite understand why cats need to spoil nice gardens with this modern art type of thing. There's neither rhyme nor reason to it. It's just plain ridiculous. Don't get me wrong – the idea of a lovely book festival is all well and good, but sticking statues up in the middle of Marcia Woolcoat's memorial gardens is plain heresy. And what a statue it is! Beryl and I haven't seen the like of it since the Lancashire witch trials pageant the year we left home to come here and set up the bakery.' Except for Poppa, Hettie and Emmeline Brontë, the assembled company was completely bewildered by Betty's tirade. Poppa stepped forward to save the day by going to fetch the abandoned sausages and black pudding, not wanting anyone to come across the charred remains of Charlene Brontë in the first light of dawn. 'Right my loves, let's have your orders – you all look like you could do with a nice big fry-up. You look like you've found a shortbread finger and lost an apple sponge!'

Bugs Anderton considered taking exception to Betty's analogy, which decried the merits of her homeland's favourite biscuit, but she thought better of it. Now was probably not the time to lock horns with the Butter sisters over their views on confectionery.

It was Beryl who noticed Bruiser first. 'By heavens, lad! What sort of a mess have you got yourself in?' she said, bustling across to his makeshift sickbed. 'I thought your fighting days were over. You're old enough to know better. Look at him, Betty – an extra sausage on his plate, I think.'

Wiping her paws on her apron, Betty joined her sister at Bruiser's bedside. 'Hot beef tea for starters. I sent some across for Mr Page, as he's particularly partial. I'll fetch it if Miss Treemints would kindly mix it with some hot water?' Delirium responded once again to the battle cry and the Butters continued to issue their own special brand of sticking plaster to the weary and shell-shocked gathering, caring little for the horrors of the night or the implications for those left standing.

The beef tea proved a real hit with Bruiser. Although weak and in pain, he brightened up sufficiently to sit in a chair, allowing Cherry and Hilary Fudge to bandage his wounds properly. The bleeding had stopped and they were able to put his damaged arm and shoulder into a sling, which delighted Cherry as she'd been wanting to put her sling-folding to good use for some time. Hilary crowned the work with a large, bright safety pin, and the two first-aiders stood back to admire their work as praise was heaped on them from every direction.

Poppa returned with the sausages and the black pudding, and reported that the festival site was awash but starting to dry out. He also discreetly informed Hettie that the 'situation' was still standing very prominently in the memorial gardens.

'We need a definite plan,' she said as the first welcome smell of the Butters' cooked breakfasts filled the air. 'I think we should have a meeting over breakfast and work out what to do next. There'll be hundreds of happy festivalgoers turning up at the gates of Furcross in a few hours' time, expecting to be entertained. If the festival is to be cancelled, we need to get the message out there somehow before there's a riot.'

With Poppa's help, Hettie pulled two of the authors' tables together and invited Mr Pushkin and Turner Page to join them for breakfast. Bruiser sat at the head of the table, and Tilly elected to help him with his food; Hettie placed herself next to Poppa at the other end, with Turner Page and Mr Pushkin in the middle. Darius Bonnet joined Bugs Anderton on a table for two and Polly Hodge presided over the rest of the company in the staff canteen area, giving Hettie the privacy she needed for her strategy meeting.

The Butter sisters had excelled themselves. Within a very short space of time, every cat in the hospitality tent was enjoying a full cooked breakfast of sausage, bacon, black pudding and eggs, finished off with a slice of Beryl's special fried bread. Even Emmeline Brontë obliged with a clean plate, although the egg stain down her nightdress did very little to enhance her celebrity. Having worked wonders on everyone else, the Butters invited Delirium Treemints to join them for a caterers' breakfast and the three cats sat behind the counter in the peace of the field kitchen while Hettie's table got down to some serious conversation.

'The storm has left a bit of a mess out there, to put it mildly,' Hettie began. 'The big question is do we continue with the festival or declare the site a disaster area and cut our losses?' All eyes turned to Turner Page, the only cat at the table who would stand to make a loss in the financial sense of the word.

Spurred on by Mr Pushkin, he spoke up. 'As the director of this festival, I stand to lose everything if I have to return the ticket money. As most of you know, we hoped to make a small profit to spend on updating our library books; the rest of the money has already been spent on publicity, authors' fees and the hiring of tents and marquee. None of these expenses are returnable, and so I fear that I will have to consider selling Furcross House to settle my debts.'

Mr Pushkin squeezed Turner's paw. 'I am sure it cannot come to this,' he said, using his Russian accent to its full potential.

'Well, let's try and stay positive,' said Hettie. 'Let's do some "what ifs".'

Tilly clapped her paws together in delight. She loved it when Hettie had one of her 'what if' sessions. The rest of the table sat in silence, waiting for Hettie's powers of reason to manifest themselves. 'What if we tidied up out there and changed the programme round a bit? Muddy Fryer's a big attraction; we still have Polly Hodge and Nicolette Upstart, and we even still have one Brontë sister. And then there's the festival band. On the face of it, the only things missing as far as today's line-up is concerned are Downton Tabby and Ann Brontë. Charlene did her bit yesterday, so she's done and dusted.'

Turner Page brightened a little, but felt he had to make the point that everyone else was thinking. 'But Downton Tabby was due to appear again today, and most of the Saturday tickets have been sold on the strength of his being here.'

Tilly responded on Hettie's behalf. 'I don't think they'll mind once they get here. Things often have to be cancelled at the last minute, and lots of cats saw him yesterday. Muddy went down a storm even before he came on, and he wasn't very nice anyway.'

Tilly's honesty often got her into hot water; this time it worked to her advantage and there was a general nod of approval around the table. Hettie continued. 'What if we front up and invite Hacky Redtop to run an exclusive in tomorrow's *Sunday Snout* on the murder of Downton Tabby and Ann Brontë? It would be the biggest story of the year. We could even let Prunella Snap take pictures.'

'Not until we've found the head,' Tilly pointed out.

Hettie agreed that the head was a bit of a problem, but pushed on with her vision. 'Instead of giving up, we could really put the festival on the map. There aren't many events that offer their own murder mysteries. If we tidied them up a bit, we could even charge for viewing the bodies.'

Turner Page shuddered at the thought but Bruiser and Poppa were fully behind Hettie, knowing that the only way out of a disaster was to make capital from it.

Poppa offered an idea of his own. 'If we could transport Charlene in her present state to the library, she'd make a great attraction with her victims around her – a sort of Furcross Black Museum touch. A bit of embalming fluid here and there, and Bob's your uncle.'

Mr Pushkin joined in, adding his penny's worth. 'In Russia, we keep our important cats going long after they die so that people can visit. It is most respectful, and people queue from morning till night to file past them. I think Miss Hettie and Mr Poppa have a very good idea to get us out of a big hole.'

The table was now alive with possibilities, and the somewhat macabre suggestion was growing wings; all they needed was Downton Tabby's head and they could be staging the greatest show on earth, or at least the most extraordinary event the town had ever hosted.

'We should try and keep the events going in the marquee,' Hettie continued. 'We need to make the cats think they've still had a good day out, and not everyone will want to check out the corpses. What if we could convince Emmeline to do a tribute to her sisters and their books? That would go down well, and Muddy could select her best murder ballads to sing.'

'And we could ask the Butters to put on Crime Teas in the marquee,' squealed Tilly, getting overexcited.

The town's clock chimed five, which served as a reminder that they had exactly five hours to plan and turn day two of the literary festival into a murder and mayhem event.

'OK, all this is going to take a lot of work, so let's have a vote on it. Paws up if you think we should go for it.' Hettie was delighted to see a unanimous vote of confidence; even Bruiser managed to indicate his enthusiasm by waving his one good paw in the air. 'That settles it then.' Hettie stifled a yawn, fighting the fact that she'd been awake for nearly twenty-four hours without so much as a catnap. 'Let's go and tell the others what we propose to do. We'll need every pair of paws we can get to pull this one off.'

153

'I can't see me bein' much help,' said Bruiser, looking disappointed at missing out on the excitement.

'You need to get some rest,' Hettie cautioned. 'If we manage to get the bodies set up in the library, you can sit and take the money with your good paw and keep an eye on things in there. I'm sure Mr Pushkin would be happy to help.'

Mr Pushkin nodded in Bruiser's direction and Hettie stood up to lead her planning committee into the staff area, where the rest of the cats waited for news.

CHAPTER ELEVEN

Hettie's plan was well-received and there was no shortage of volunteers. Turner Page was elected to put in various telephone calls to the local newspaper office and the town's undertakers. It promised to be another very hot day and it was vital that the bodies on display should be at least presentable and show no sign of deterioration throughout the viewing time. Hettie, Poppa and Darius Bonnet were on body removal and head search, a task vital to the success of the plan, and all the remaining cats were sent out to effect a clean-up and tidy session of the festival grounds. Tilly had appointed herself stage manager of the events marquee, and began re-jigging the running order before approaching the authors and musicians individually to discuss her new programme.

The Butter sisters wiped their surfaces down from breakfast, tidied the field kitchen, and returned to their bakery via Mr Tiddles' taxi to begin the pies and pastries required for a new day. Under the circumstances, Tilly had suggested that there should be three themed options to the catering: Murder Munches for lunch; Crime Teas in the afternoon; and Deadly Dinners for those who wished to stay on into the evening. Betty and Beryl were pleased to oblige by dreaming up some new fillings to wrap their famous pastry around, agreeing to serve the three meal sessions in the events marquee between performances. It was decided that Delirium Treemints would remain in hospitality to dispense beverages and snacks to the festival staff and artists throughout the day.

The cats all scattered to their various tasks. Bugs Anderton, keen to retrieve her organisational status, led Hilary and Cherry Fudge out into the early morning to gather the detritus left by the storm into large, black dustbin bags. Hettie, Poppa and Darius set about the unenviable task of transporting the bodies from their temporary resting places to the library. Mr Pushkin had suggested the biology and science section, and had gone ahead to build a makeshift dais to display the macabre tableau. As crime writers, Polly Hodge and Nicolette Upstart were more interested in the bodies; they followed Hettie and her team out of the

156

tent at a discreet distance to observe, each in the hope of finding a decent plot for her next book.

'Let's start with Charlene Brontë,' said Hettie. 'She's going to be the most difficult one to move, and we need to get her set up first.'

They splashed their way across to the memorial garden and stared in wonder at the blackened form which now dominated what had once been a peaceful place. The broadsword that had proved her undoing was propping her up, her paws still clutching the hilt, the point sunk into the ground. Poppa returned to the tent to fetch the wheelbarrow while Hettie and Darius took a closer look at the job.

'Tricky,' said Hettie. 'We need to make sure nothing falls off, and I think the sword will have to come with her – it looks like her paws are welded to it.'

Fighting back the revulsion he felt at the sight before him, Darius offered a suggestion. 'I had to shift a giant statue once from Sir Downton's country house,' he said. 'It was wearing a full suit of armour and weighed a ton. We rocked it onto a big trolley and dragged it round to the kitchen garden.' Poppa had returned with the wheelbarrow and agreed that a spot of gentle rocking might free the sword from the ground, releasing the body for transportation. Hettie placed herself behind the corpse to steady it as Poppa and Darius began to rock. The body stood firm after several attempts, then finally gave way, falling backwards onto Hettie. She lay pinned to the ground by the blackened effigy, and an acrid smell rose in her nostrils as she fought to push the horror away from her. Poppa and Darius responded quickly and lifted the body high enough for Hettie to roll away. The puddle she found herself lying in was a great comfort after the close proximity of the charred remains.

Wringing out the hem of her T-shirt, Hettie struggled to her feet and the three cats lifted the body into the wheelbarrow, taking care not to dislodge the sword or inadvertently break off any limbs. The strange cortège made its way through the marquee and out the other side, with Poppa pushing and Hettie and Darius either side as a guard of honour. Polly and Nicolette followed in hot pursuit, but lost interest as soon as Nicolette discovered that her pop-up stall had become a murder site. Fascinated by the bloodstained puddles that surrounded it, Nicolette raised her stall to its full height, checking that her stock was still safe in the storage pockets. There was no damage as far as she could see, but the stock was a little damp so she set about laying it out in the surrounding borders to dry in the early morning sun. Polly Hodge pulled a notepad from her large handbag and started making furious notes, taking in every detail. It was no secret in the book world that the celebrated crime author was currently looking for inspiration, and – judging by the satisfied look on her face – she had now found it.

Mr Pushkin had been very busy in their absence. By the time Poppa barged open the French windows to the library with the wheelbarrow, he'd created a small stage and covered it in a pair of purple velvet curtains that he and Turner had disagreed on in their private accommodation.

'Perfect,' said Hettie. 'Just the right tone, I think. Let's get her up there as the centrepiece. We'll decide on where to put the others when we see how she looks.'

With Mr Pushkin directing, Hettie, Poppa and Darius lifted the corpse into the centre of the dais, propping her up on the broadsword which stood out in front of her.

'Magnificent!' declared Hettie as they stood back to admire their work. 'It's Joan of Arc all over again. Any news on the undertaker?'

'Mr Shroud and Mr Trestle are sending Morbid Balm to tidy them up,' said Mr Pushkin. 'She's got a special spray to keep the flies off,' he continued cheerfully. 'And Turner's arranged for Hacky Redtop and Prunella Snap to drop in at about nine to take pictures and get the story for the *Sunday Snout*.'

'We'd better get a move on, then,' Hettie said, trying not to think about Morbid Balm and her fly spray. 'Let's do the camper van next – that should be an easy one. Poppa and I can manage that on our own, Darius – maybe you could have a quick look for the missing head now it's light?'

Darius shrank back at the thought, but recovered quickly when he realised that it was his chance to perform a final service for his dead master. The three cats left the library as Polly Hodge arrived to admire their handiwork so far.

No one had taken much notice of Emmeline Brontë during the conversations and activity to save the festival. She sat wrapped in a tablecloth, staring into space, with her tea only sipped at. Tilly looked up from her newly drawn stage plan, knowing that Emmeline would now be a star attraction: not only was she the last Brontë standing, but of all three sisters she was the most popular. The problem was how to convince her to take part after all that had happened; suggesting that she offer a tribute to her dead sisters when they had both abused her might prove to be a little out of order. It had to be done, though, and there was no time like the present.

Tilly put down her pencil and made her way to Emmeline's table. 'You look all in,' she said, adopting a sympathetic approach. 'Maybe you should go and have a nice sleep? I can arrange for your things to be moved to your sister Ann's old room. If you have a rest, you'll be fresh for your event later – lots of cats are coming to see you today and you'll be playing to a packed house.'

Remarkably, Emmeline responded well to Tilly's encouragement. 'Your words are of great kindness,

160

and I shall be pleased to rest. It is my wish to see the festival through before returning to Porkshire, where my spirit shall be lighter.'

Avoiding any further discussion regarding Emmeline's more ethereal tendencies, Tilly left her in the capable paws of Delirium Treemints and made her way across to the accommodation block, where Poppa and Hettie had just arrived with the wheelbarrow. 'One down and two to go,' said Hettie by way of greeting. 'How's the line-up coming along?'

'Better than expected. Emmeline has agreed to do her event. I've just got to sort out her room so that she can have a lie-down. She looks dreadful.'

'Nowhere near as bad as her sisters,' Hettie observed wryly. 'I'll come with you. I need to get the keys to the camper – we'll have to unlock the back doors to get flat-packed Ann out.' Both Tilly and Poppa collapsed in peals of laughter. Clearly tiredness was taking its toll. Any amount of black humour served to lift their spirits, and Hettie could be relied upon to keep her off-colour quips coming.

In daylight, the room that Charlene Brontë had shared with Emmeline resembled a chamber of horrors. There were bloodstains everywhere, and the bed piled high with hastily discarded clothes offered enough evidence to condemn Charlene ten times over; it was very clear that she had held Emmeline captive in the other bed, but why?

'This is a sorry state of affairs,' said Hettie, picking her way through the bloodied clothes until she found the keys to the camper van. 'Maybe Emmeline knew that her sister was planning to kill Downton Tabby and tried to stop her. Perhaps Ann found out and had to be silenced as well. What I can't understand, though, is why Charlene would stick around like some bloody half-crazed serial killer. Why didn't she fire up the camper and get the hell out after her little killing spree?'

'I don't think she can drive,' said Tilly. 'Emmeline does all the driving. She told me how tired she was because she'd driven from Porkshire.'

Hettie shrugged her shoulders. 'Oh well, at least we have our murderer, even if she is burnt to a crisp. And maybe Emmeline will be up to answering a few questions later. It's still all a bit of a mystery – and why did Charlene kill Downton Tabby? That's the big one.'

'Well, I'd rather you didn't ask too many questions until Emmeline has done her event,' said Tilly, collecting the suitcase closest to Emmeline's bed. 'She's my star turn for our murder and mayhem day, and I wouldn't want her getting more upset than she is already.'

Tilly struggled out into the corridor with the suitcase and unlocked the room that Ann Brontë had so briefly occupied. She cleared Ann's things to one side and did her best to make the room welcoming.

Hettie took the camper's keys out into the car park, where Poppa was waiting to perform yet another grim task with the wheelbarrow.

'Flat-packed Ann', as Hettie had christened her, proved a much easier corpse to move. Hettie unbuckled the straps and let down the bunk bed, and together they slid the body off the bed and into the wheelbarrow. In death, Ann Brontë was by no means the showpiece her sister had become; her dark raven fur was squashed and spiky in places, and there was an unpleasant scent coming from her.

'The sooner Morbid Balm gets here, the better,' said Hettie, shutting the back doors to the camper van. 'Poor Ann needs a bit of a makeover before she goes on display.'

Poppa agreed and the two cats wheeled the body towards the library, much to the delight of Polly Hodge, who greeted them at the French windows and started a new page in her notepad, thrilled to have another body to focus on.

CHAPTER TWELVE

'Morbid Balm, at your service,' said the cheerful, round-faced cat as Hettie and Poppa wheeled Ann Brontë into the library. 'Some folks like to call me Miss M. Balm as their little joke, on account of my chosen profession, but I don't mind because it keeps things cheery. That's what I do – cheer things up. Now, what have we got here?'

Hettie was a little taken aback by the opening speech from Shroud and Trestle's employee, but she could see instantly that Morbid Balm would be a wonderful asset in times of crisis. She was dressed mainly in black but wore an abundance of jewellery: a string of giant pearls around her neck; several rings on her painted red claws; and a multitude of bangles marching up both her arms, which clattered every time she moved. She looked a little out of place in her tall, lace-up boots and a black skirt which hung in jagged black satin petals around her.

'We have three bodies to put on display,' Hettie began. 'The one you see on the dais over there, this one in the wheelbarrow, and another one which hasn't arrived yet.'

Morbid shot a look in the direction of the dais. 'Well, I'm not being funny or anything, but I can't do a lot for that one. No hair to brush, see? Those teeth won't whiten up, either, but I could pop a couple of glass eyes in her sockets if you like? It *is* a she, isn't it?'

Hettie nodded as Morbid fell to her knees to take a closer look in the wheelbarrow. 'I can help with this one, though. She looks a bit flat but I could puff her fur up a bit and even put a smile on her face if you didn't mind me breaking her jaw – looks a bit set in its ways just now.'

'I think we need to keep the expression the way it is. She did die a nasty death and a smile might not be the right way to go.' Hettie marvelled at how easily she had slipped into the matter-of-fact discussion on after-death makeovers. 'Eyes might be good for the other one, though.'

Morbid responded by snapping the catches open on her large, wheeled suitcase, which revealed the tools of her trade – compartment after compartment, all neatly

166

labelled. 'What colour were they?' she asked, pulling open a draw labelled 'eyes'.

'I'm not too sure, but this cat in the wheelbarrow is her sister,' said Hettie, staring at the glass eyes as they stared back at her.

'Let's have a look, then.' Morbid wasted no time in lifting one of Ann Brontë's eyelids. 'Black as pitch. I've run out of them, but I do have a novelty line that might be just right for your purpose.' Morbid opened another drawer in her case marked 'Special effects'. 'How about these?'

Hettie, Poppa and Mr Pushkin gathered round as Morbid pulled a pair of seemingly straightforward glass globes from the drawer. 'Them's me rainbow prisms,' she said, holding them up to the light.

Shocked and delighted in equal measure, Hettie had to agree that the eyeballs did look very striking when they were lit up and would probably enhance the horrific aspects of the display very nicely.

'I got fluorescent whiskers as well, if you like, but that might be overkill.'

Hettie resisted Morbid's glow-in-the-dark range, knowing that time was passing and the display was by no means complete, mainly due to the absence of Downton Tabby and his head. 'I think I'll leave you to it, then, Miss . . . er . . . Morbid. Mr Pushkin here will assist you in any way he can. If you could tidy Ann up and fill Charlene's sockets, that would be lovely.'

Poppa and Mr Pushkin unloaded the wheelbarrow, laying Ann Brontë on a nearby table as Morbid Balm plugged in her hairdryer and gathered her combs and brushes from the suitcase. 'How are you going to display this one? Do you want her looking nice all round or just from the front?'

Hettie hadn't really thought that far ahead, but a decision had to be made. 'I think perhaps we could have her sitting in a chair, looking frightened.'

'With a look on her face like the one she's got now, that won't be a problem. I'll have to see what I can do about the sitting position, though. Like I said before, she *is* a bit flat.'

'Excellent,' said Hettie, nodding to Poppa and grabbing the empty wheelbarrow. 'We'll go and fetch the other body and leave you to get on.'

The day was already warm as Hettie and Poppa stepped out into the sunlight. Looking around the stalls area, they could see that Bugs Anderton and her helpers had done wonders in their clean-up session. The bunting had been rehung, the rubbish scattered by the storm was neatly bagged, and even some of the giant puddles were beginning to dry up. The early sun made everything sparkle, and, for the first time in twelve hours, Hettie felt hopeful about what the day might bring.

'I suppose we'd better catch up with Darius Bonnet,' she said, wheeling the barrow into the marquee. 'I wonder if he's had any luck with the missing head? It's got to be somewhere around here.'

Tilly was on the stage, rearranging chairs, and Muddy Fryer seemed to have collapsed in a heap on top of her Round Table, snatching some much-needed rest. 'Have you seen Darius?' whispered Hettie, tiptoeing past the singer.

'Not recently. How's the display going?' asked Tilly, sticking her new running order to the tent flap.

'The good news is that Morbid Balm has arrived and is giving Ann Brontë a makeover, but we still have to shift Downton Tabby and that's obviously a bit of a problem. Where are the rest of them?'

'Bugs and the Fudges are clearing up the memorial garden, Nicolette is sponging down her pop-up and Bruiser is asleep in Miss Scarlet's sidecar. I've delivered Emmeline to Ann's room so she can have a rest. Muddy's over there on her table, and Polly Hodge is right behind you with her notepad.'

Hettie turned on her heel as the author bore down on her. 'Miss Bagshot, you must return to the library immediately. We have visitors from breakfast television!'

'Well, that's all I bloody need! How the hell did they get wind of anything? We've promised the exclusive to the *Sunday Snout*. Have they seen anything yet?'

'Not as far as I know. Mr Pushkin is holding them at bay in the front car park and asked me to fetch you.'

Hettie strode out of the marquee and bumped straight into Meridian Hambone, who had arrived early with more festival T-shirts. 'Mornin'! I thought I'd get me pitch set up before any of them others arrive. I just done some business out front already. Them TV types is all wearin' me "Littertrays" now. Any chance of me 'avin' a bite to eat in yer staff canteen when I've set this lot up?'

Hettie didn't answer, but pushed past Meridian and her boxes, keen to fight off the media attack which awaited her in the driveway of Furcross House. On reaching the library, she noticed that the air was filled with a sweet-smelling scent, and Morbid Balm was obviously using her spray to great effect. Hettie glanced up at what was left of Charlene Brontë and noticed that the glass eyes were already in place, shining out like laser beams in every direction and giving the dead cat the look of a Hollywood comic-strip hero. It wasn't perhaps the look she'd envisaged, but it was impressive all the same. Morbid herself was hard at work, blow-drying Ann Brontë's fur.

The library resembled the sort of madhouse which only manifested itself in the best nightmares, but nothing could have prepared Hettie for the performance she was about to get involved in up to her elegant tabby neck. Mr Pushkin was standing his ground at the entrance to Furcross House. The TV team – all sporting Meridian's 'Littertray' T-shirts – was milling around with wires and cameras, all being unloaded from their broadcast van. In the middle of the chaos stood two cats whom Hettie recognised instantly, although she was rarely awake to see them present their local TV breakfast show. Evil Simmonds and her colleague, Spiro Hunch, had been a duo to be reckoned with in their time: Evil had fronted the nation's top investigative show, *Catarama*, for many years until her unfortunate downfall over a catnip-for-questions incident; Spiro was lucky to have a job at all after news broke of his penchant for kittens, but money was paid and silence bought.

'Miss Simmonds,' said Hettie, moving forward, 'what brings you here at this time of day? I'm not aware of your having booked an appointment today.'

Evil Simmonds turned her eye on Hettie, looking her up and down before replying. 'We go where the news takes us. And you are?'

Hettie's hackles rose instantly, but it suddenly occurred to her that her dishevelled appearance was doing her no favours with the media. Her *Lord of the Pies* T-shirt was covered in mud, blood and various bits of food from the hospitality tent, and it was no wonder that the broadcaster had been so dismissive. 'I am Hettie Bagshot from the No. 2 Feline Detective Agency, and I am in charge of security here at the festival. As you can see, we have had a difficult night with the storm but those of us on-site are working hard to clean up before the festivalgoers arrive at ten.'

Evil Simmonds smiled, revealing a set of perfect white teeth. 'Well, you've answered your own question, haven't you? We're here because of the storm. It's caused havoc in the town. Greasy Tom's van has been washed away, Elsie Haddock's fish and chip shop has been flooded, Malkin and Sprinkle's food hall is an inch deep in water, and the river is ready to burst its banks. We're here to see if today's festival is going ahead, so if you could find me a cat who would look good on camera, we'll do them and move on.'

Hettie could have hugged the presenter, and the relief must have shown in her face. Of course! It was the *storm* that was the story, and not – as she had first suspected – the death of Downton Tabby. 'Oh dear, that all sounds terrible,' she said, putting on her concerned face. 'Perhaps you would like to talk to one of our festival stars? I could offer you P. D. Hodge or Nicolette Upstart – or Miss Muddy Fryer, who was unable to continue to another festival after her performance here last night because of the storm.'

'What about Downton Tabby?' asked Spiro Hunch, joining in the conversation. 'He's my favourite, and he's a much bigger star than the rest of 'em put together.'

For a moment, Hettie couldn't avoid her rabbit-in-headlights stance, but she quickly recovered herself.

'Dear me, it's more than my job's worth to disturb Sir Downton at this time of the morning, especially after such an unsettled night.'

'Well, that's a pity. I hear he's been headhunted by the other channel for a new series. Any truth in that?' Spiro continued.

The very mention of heads threw Hettie into an uncharacteristic stutter. 'Er . . . well . . . er . . . no, not to my knowledge. I'm just security, though, and who knows what these stars are up to? Not my department, really. I think . . .'

Hettie's ramblings were interrupted by Morbid Balm, who'd forced herself past Mr Pushkin with some urgency. 'I can do replacement eyes, whiskers and expressions, but replacement heads! Not my thing, really, and he'll need another suit of clothes if he's to look respect . . .'

Hettie lunged at Morbid, wrapping her in a hug that constricted her breathing while Evil Simmonds and Spiro Hunch looked on. 'Morbid, how lovely of you to come and help with the clean-up! Morbid has been fixing some of the festival displays that were damaged in the storm,' she explained, steering the Goth cat back towards the door of Furcross House. 'I don't want to be rude, but we still have a lot to do here and time is ticking on.'

It was Polly Hodge who saved the day by appearing at exactly the right moment. Evil Simmonds, who recognised the author immediately, went into broadcast mode and began with a piece to camera, introducing their location ready for handing over to Spiro, who was bearing down on the famous crime writer.

'For God's sake, just stick to the storm, stay off the murders and send them away happy,' whispered Hettie, pushing Morbid towards the door. Polly Hodge nodded, and beamed at Spiro in a 'Let me tell you about my latest book' sort of way.

When Hettie reached the library, the scene before her was perhaps the most bizarre that she had ever witnessed. Morbid Balm had worked wonders on Ann Brontë. Her corpse sat next to the malevolent figure of her blackened sister, her mouth wide in a horrific grimace and her fur shiny and fluffed up, as if she'd been electrocuted and was still connected to the power source. The body at the foot of the dais lay awkwardly in the wheelbarrow which Poppa had just retrieved from the hospitality tent, and was the cause of Morbid's untimely intervention.

'No sign of Darius, so I thought I'd bring Sir Downton over,' he said. 'Delirium Treemints said it wasn't good to have it in a food preparation area, and anyway it was making her feel sick.'

Hettie stared down at the corpse. The bloodstained checked suit looked ridiculous without a head. 'See what I mean?' said Morbid. 'He's not going to fit in with the other two like that. Is there some sort of story to all of this? If there is, it's an odd sort of tale.'

Hettie had to agree, but was grateful that Morbid's pride in her work prevented her from delving too deeply into what had happened to the bodies in the first place. 'We're searching for the rest of him, and I'm sure things will look much better when we've found the head,' she said apologetically, more to herself than to the undertaker. 'Why don't you have a break? There's food and drink in our hospitality tent.'

'All right, but I'll have to be gone by nine. We got two funerals and a cremation later, and I got a wig to fit and three to dress before we send them on their way – but a nice cup of tea and a bun wouldn't go amiss after me early start.'

Leaving Poppa to guard the library from unwanted intruders, Hettie led the way, stopping to purchase a couple of festival T-shirts from Meridian Hambone, who'd laid out her stall and was now forcing a festival doughnut into her mouth. 'You'll 'ave to 'elp yerself, cos I'm covered in sugar,' she said, clawing the money into the pouch of an old apron she always wore.

Tilly was standing by the bookstall as Hettie and Morbid approached. 'Is there anything I can do? I've sorted the new running order. Looks like being a good show.'

'You can change into one of these,' said Hettie, pushing a T-shirt at her. 'Your *Fur in the Sunlight* looks more like *Matted at Midnight*. It's time we cleaned ourselves up a bit.'

Tilly loved new clothes and pounced on the T-shirt. Most of her wardrobe came from Jessie's charity shop, and although the garments were of good quality, there was nothing nicer than brand new, even if it did have 'Littertray' written all over it. The three cats entered the marquee, tiptoeing past a snoring Muddy Fryer and out the other side. Hettie marvelled at the transformation which Bugs and her team had achieved in the memorial gardens. Hilary and Cherry Fudge had extended their first-aid talents to the flower and shrub borders, dead heading the storm-damaged bedding plants, while Bugs had spent some time up a wobbly ladder, reattaching a climbing rose to its trellis. The puddles were still quite deep in places, but Hettie, Morbid and Tilly picked their way across to hospitality without any problem.

Betty and Beryl Butter had returned from their high street bakery bursting with news and freshly baked pies and pastries, and were holding court as they filled the canteen's service area with the fruits of their labours.

'High street's awash! We haven't seen anything like it since the avalanche ran down Pendle Hill, have we, Betty?' said Beryl, unloading a tray of flapjacks onto the counter.

'Poor Elsie Haddock's got her mop out,' Betty

176

continued, 'and as for Lavender Stamp's post office – we left her wringing out her hand-knitted dolls. You know – the ones she sells as extras to her stamps and postal orders.' Hettie nodded. It was general knowledge that the postmistress spent her lonely winter evenings knitting life-size male cats to fill the void in her life after being jilted by Laxton Sprat, a cat who had dallied with her affections before taking himself off to university many years before. Lavender had turned her back on romance, and had taken instead to creating the perfect male in rows of knit one purl one, which she sold in the post office once she had tired of them.

'What about the bakery?' Hettie asked, fearing for their own back room on the premises.

'No problem our side of the street. There's a bit of collateral damage to Beryl's hollyhocks but that's about it.'

Hettie breathed a sigh of relief and slumped down on the nearest chair. Delirium brought across a tray of teas and doughnuts, and Tilly and Morbid pounced on the food as if they hadn't eaten for a week. Hettie hugged her cup of tea and allowed a wash of tiredness to engulf her for a few minutes. There was still much to do, and finding Downton Tabby's head had become critical to the day's success.

It was just as well that Tilly had refrained from changing into her new T-shirt until after the doughnuts.

The jam that ran through them extended its journey across the old one, almost obliterating any sign of a book title. She marvelled at how Morbid was able to keep her doughnut under control without the slightest damage to her gothic look, and made a mental note to try to keep her clothes cleaner for longer.

The tea break was over, and Hettie had barely nibbled at her doughnut. She was exhausted and troubled by the macabre turn which the festival had been forced to take. Was it tiredness or fear which had made this scene of carnage an acceptable possibility? Displays of horror were nothing new in feline culture, but this was different: only a few hours ago, Downton Tabby was blustering his way through a book event; Charlene and Ann Brontë were using the militant side of their characters to create a spark that all potentially dull authors needed; and Emmeline drifted between two worlds, seemingly untouched by either. Now, three of them had been united in a grotesque tableau of death which would probably entertain and thrill far more than their books and TV shows could ever do.

Tilly had clearly found a new friend in Morbid Balm, who was delighting her with funereal stories as the doughnuts were succeeded by freshly baked sausage rolls. The Butters had turned the small field kitchen into a haven of expectation as they struggled to fill large catering pans with the ingredients for the day's themed meals, and it occurred to Hettie that the hospitality tent had become a retreat from the seemingly unending chaos which existed outside its bubble of contentment. But it was time to make a move. She discarded her *Lord of the Pies* T-shirt and struggled into the new one, feeling better instantly. It was as if the night's bloody work had been washed away, to be replaced by a new beginning. She stood up and strode out into the sunlight, determined to make the day a success.

CHAPTER THIRTEEN

By half past eight, the stalls area outside the events marquee was a hubbub of cats and gossip, mostly led by Nicolette Upstart, who was delighting her fellow stallholders with a lurid and detailed account of the murders. Even the Green Peas and Cats of the Earth stalls had buried their differences and integrated themselves into the market society which was now blossoming. Tilly's friend Jessie had added a selection of hand-painted wellingtons to her barrow, knowing that they would be an instant hit with festivalgoers. As soon as the storm struck the town, Jessie had left the comfort of her bed and – with a little help from a pipe or two of catnip – spent the rest of the night creating psychedelic masterpieces from the plain, dull mountain of second-hand wellingtons which had accumulated in her charity shop over the winter.

As word spread about the murders, Nicolette realised she had missed a trick by washing Downton Tabby's blood from her pop-up stall. In hindsight, she could have offered it as a gory murder exhibit for the crime fiction fans who would besiege the festival once the gates to Furcross were opened at ten. As it was, most of the night's terror had been contained on the small dais in the library, and except for a crumpled bunk bed in the Brontë's camper van, there was very little to show of Charlene's deadly rampage.

Mr Chapter and Mr Spine had had a terrible journey in from Southwool. The festival's booksellers had driven their van through deep water, moved fallen trees, and been stuck in mud twice before they reached Furcross. Their shop, which took up a prime position on the seafront, had escaped the flooding by a whisker, thanks to Mr Chapter's speedy response to a threateningly high sea. Living over the shop, he'd acted quickly, piling the shop doorway with the sandbags that were kept in the book overspill shed for such emergencies. His neighbours had not been so diligent, and it was with a certain smugness that he drove off to collect Mr Spine that morning, while the other seafront shopkeepers busied themselves with mops, buckets and damaged stock.

Their three trestle tables had withstood the battering of the storm, and the thick waterproof tarpaulins with which they'd covered the books had only leaked in a couple of places. They lifted and folded the covers in a methodical display of synchronisation as their fellow stallholders looked on. Then – with barely a second glance at the books – they headed for the hospitality tent for a much needed breakfast.

It was Jessie who noticed first. Having set out her stall, she wandered across to browse the books. The festival authors were prominent, with the Brontës taking centre stage on the middle trestle table, flanked by P. D. Hodge and Nicolette Upstart. On the table to the right, there were collections of signed copies from romantic novelists: Mavis Binky stood out, along with her arch and very pink rival Barbara Catland, and then came the latest books from Terry Scratchit and J. K. Roll-on, both leading the bestseller lists in the art of fantasy writing. Jessie loved anything with a wizard or a ghost in it, and she decided to treat herself later in the day if her decorated wellingtons were a success.

The final table groaned under the weight of Downton Tabby's efforts, and it was here that Jessie paused, then froze, then let out a high-pitched cry which could easily have woken all the cats buried in the memorial gardens. Hettie was on her way out of the library at the time and was the first to reach Jessie's side. Together, they stared open-mouthed at the display before them. There was no doubt that this was a unique and innovative way to sell books, and a passer-by might be inclined to offer nothing more than a smile, having no idea about what he was actually looking at. Downton Tabby's head sat squarely in the middle of a mountain of his books, with a cigar jammed in his mouth and his monocle placed in front of his right eye. The cat's head showed no signs of its gory detachment from its body, and could have easily been one of the plaster dummies that Jessie used to display her cloche hats.

'Well, Charlene Brontë certainly missed her vocation,' said Hettie, stepping forward to take a closer look. 'She should have gone into window dressing and display – or maybe a job at Madame Tussaud's would have suited her.'

Jessie laughed nervously. 'At least you can finish your tableau now.'

Hettie nodded. 'Yes, and just in time. Morbid Balm has started to pack her kit away. I'd better deliver this to her so that she can finish the job.' She lifted the head from its nest of books and carried it at arm's length into the library by its ears. Jessie tidied the books, removing two that were particularly bloodstained; no doubt when the story broke, those particular copies would sell for huge prices to the collectors of murder relics, but it was a trade that Jessie had no time for.

'I could stitch it back on,' said Morbid, enthusing over the head in the library. 'It depends what sort of effect you want. The rest of him needs a change of clothes, unless you want the bloodstains as a feature. The head looks quite respectable as it is, really. We could just stick it on a plate and put it in Ann Brontë's lap and not bother with the rest of him, or we could make up an old-fashioned block to make it look like an execution – head one side, body the other. That would look good with the broadsword.'

Hettie shook her head. 'To be honest, Morbid, as long as it draws the crowds I couldn't care less. There needs to be a vague statement, like murderer and victims, but I'll leave the rest of it up to you.'

Hettie turned on her heel and walked back out into the sunshine, leaving Morbid Balm to her work. Tilly had joined Jessie by her stall and was admiring the painted wellingtons as Hettie approached. 'Got the head just in time then,' she said.

'Yes. I've left Morbid to decide where to stick it. Are we all set in the events marquee?' Tilly nodded, and glanced across at the tent just as Muddy Fryer emerged, looking like she'd spent three days longer than everyone else at a rather good party. The sunlight blinded her for a moment, causing her to crash into Nicolette's pop-up, but she bounced off it and offered her apologies. Finally able to focus, she made a beeline for Jessie's stall. 'Nice wellies,' she said, admiring the new stock. 'As I'm stayin' on to do the murder ballads, I was wonderin' if you could sell me tapes again? I'll have to fetch some more from me van if I can find the cricket field. And I ought to get me Arthurian stuff shifted before the crowds descend. Do you know if me sword's turned up yet?'

Both Tilly and Jessie shot a look at Hettie, indicating that she had been chosen to field that particular enquiry. Hettie responded by taking Muddy's paw and leading her back into the library. The singer gasped at the dais. 'Oh my word! You don't do things by halves round here, do you? They *are* all dead, aren't they? Not just clever make-up? I got this friend who sprays herself with gold paint and stands on a box all day not moving a muscle. She makes more than I do singin' me songs, but she goes through hell when it's time to comb the paint out of her fur. Even when she's clean, she's got gold highlights. Still, you'd have to pay a fortune for them these days. I once had highlights, but they'd turned purple by the third day of the tour and I had to wear a mummer's mask for the rest of the gigs to cover them up.'

Hettie realised that she could listen to Muddy

186

Fryer all day if she had the time. Like her songs, her conversation always had a strong story running through it, but now Hettie was more concerned with convincing the singer that her precious broadsword was the only thing propping up Charlene Brontë's body, and that to remove it would be a catastrophe. She'd hoped to enlist Morbid's support but the undertaker had become totally star-struck in the presence of Muddy Fryer, whose tales of death and destruction had become the soundtrack to her life, possibly even encouraging her to take up a career with Shroud and Trestle. Hettie stared at the tableau for a moment, and chose her words carefully. 'The thing is, your sword has vanquished a murderer – and for that reason it should be displayed to its full potential. We'll be taking the whole thing down later, but if we could borrow the sword until then, we could even pay you a small hire charge.'

Muddy tilted her head to one side, taking in the details of the scene before her. Morbid had positioned Downton Tabby's torso at the feet of Ann Brontë, while the towering figure of Charlene dominated the scene. 'It's a bit like the ballad of the Elric Knight,' she said, 'except it was a hand he cut off. More dramatic to have the head, though. I might sing that one later – seems appropriate with what you've got goin' on here.' Muddy skipped into a sunbeam that had just hit the library floor and began to sing:

At midnight mark the moon upstart
And the knight walked up and down,
While loudest cracks of thunder roared
Out over the hill so brown,
And in the twinkling of an eye
He spied an armed knight,
A gay lady bearing the sword,
His armour shining bright

A small but appreciative audience had now gathered in the library. Poppa and Mr Pushkin arrived fresh from waving off Evil Simmonds and her TV crew; Polly Hodge was tapping along from the crime section, where she seemed to have set up her own observation desk; and Morbid seemed to be involved in some sort of gothic step dance, parading Downton Tabby's head around the room and bringing it to rest on Ann Brontë's lap as Muddy reached the conclusion of her ballad:

And Sir Colvin has taken the bloody hand,
And set before the King,
And the morn it was on Wednesday
When he married his daughter Jean

Muddy bowed to her audience, which had grown in size during the song, and now Jessie, Tilly and Nicolette stood at the French windows, lured over by the singer's beautiful voice.

Poppa and Mr Pushkin invited Muddy to join them for breakfast, with a promise that Poppa would move her Arthurian props and escort her to the cricket field afterwards to reunite her with her van. The three cats left the library as Turner Page appeared with Hacky Redtop and Prunella Snap from the local paper. Hettie would dearly have loved to take a picture of their faces as they stared at the scene before them. Morbid, having no appetite for anything remotely connected to the media, packed her kit up and beat a hasty retreat, promising to send her bill when she got round to it.

Hacky was a seasoned newspaper cat, who had worked for all the big national dailies before setting up his own evening and Sunday papers in the town. He had turned his paw to every sort of print journalism, from working in war zones to becoming a celebrated theatre critic, although he regarded those particular jobs as having more in common than most cats would think. Prunella Snap had fallen from grace as a photographer due to some careless and unprofessional mishaps with her Olympus Trip, but Hacky had recognised her talent, and his forgiving nature and encouragement had made her an important part of his operation. Today, the shock on their faces was worth the front page of any cat's money.

'Miss Bagshot, I wonder if you might be happy to . . . er . . . fill Mr Redtop in with the details of

the new direction the festival has been forced to take?'
said Turner, taking in the full impact of the display
for the first time. Giving Hettie no chance to respond,
he strode out through the French windows, mumbling
something about breakfast.

Prunella, having got over the shock, began to
photograph the tableau from every angle, precariously
balancing herself on a library chair to take a close-up
of Charlene Brontë's blackened head and laser eyes.
By the time she'd finished, she was certain of having
several shots worthy of the *Sunday Snout*'s front page,
as well as a hefty pictorial gallery for an inside spread.

Polly Hodge had invited Hettie and Hacky Redtop
into her makeshift research area in the library so
that they could 'discuss the situation in private', then
perched herself on the edge of the desk to take in every
word and description on offer. Hettie had decided to
stick to the absolute facts of the case, and she recounted
the night's events as they had unfolded. In no time at
all, Hacky had filled ten pages of his notebook and
was keen to return to his office to prepare a special
Saturday evening edition, as well as going big on the
Sunday Snout.

The crowds were beginning to build at the gates
to Furcross House when Hettie waved Hacky and
Prunella on their way. She was pleased to have the
story released into the public domain and, in years to
come, the Furcross Literary Murders would be studied

by authors, agents and publishers alike as an example of how greed, fame and jealousy could collide with the most horrific results. For now, for her own peace of mind, Hettie was keen to find answers to some of the questions that still lingered in her mind. With most of the protagonists dead, it was going to be a difficult case to solve to her own satisfaction.

CHAPTER FOURTEEN

Penny Stone-Cragg should have retired years ago, but she was a cat who would never be suited to twilight years of gardening and knitting. She was one of the most prestigious literary agents in the country and had her well-manicured claws in every aspect of the publishing industry, including a small but lucrative publishing house of her own which flourished by picking up titles from long-dead authors and reprinting them at a price most cats could afford. Her classics range, as she liked to call it, gave her a specialisation which was rare in an agent-publisher; most of her rivals subscribed to an 'out of print, out of mind' policy, preferring to sign up young and talented writers for very small advances and derisory royalties.

Penny's living authors all had a certain amount of celebrity status: the Brontë sisters were a phenomenon she couldn't resist, and the fact that they'd completed manuscripts which had lain untouched for over a century added an extra spark of interest for her and the wider public. She had also handled the affairs of Downton Tabby in the early days of his success, negotiating his first TV deal, but an acrimonious parting of the ways severed their professional relationship. These days, with her health failing, Penny had resolved not to take on any more clients. The Brontës kept her as busy as she wanted to be, and now that her asthma attacks were becoming more frequent, charging round the country to attend her authors' events had become a little too much for her. She was making an exception this weekend and had decided to attend the second day of the festival – not to support her own authors, but to cast a curious eye across Downton Tabby now that he was at the height of his celebrity.

The wheezing had started as soon as she'd got into her car, and the four-hour journey from her home in Porkshire did nothing to improve her general state of health. The combination of hot weather and an author's event could prove a deadly cocktail, and it was with great relief that she eventually swung her Morris Minor convertible into the driveway of Furcross House, amid a sea of excited cats filing past Lavender Stamp's ticket tent. Lavender herself had only just arrived after her mop-up operation at the post office, and she was in no mood for the likes of Penny Stone-Cragg.

'Just one moment,' she said, approaching the Morris. 'You can't bring that vehicle in here. The signage is clearly marked at the bottom of Sheba Gardens. You'll have to turn round and go back the way you came, then turn left. The cricket field isn't far. Have you got a ticket? Because if you haven't, you may as well go home now. We are completely sold out for today's events.'

Penny Stone-Cragg sat in her car, gripping the steering wheel and waiting for Lavender to complete her welcome speech. She was more than capable of dealing with a jobsworth, and she calmly allowed her breathing to become a little more normal before offering Lavender some good advice. Adjusting her driving glasses to the end of her nose, she began. 'I don't have a ticket because I don't need one. I won't be leaving my car on a cricket field, because it suits me to park here. And furthermore, if it wasn't for my authors, you wouldn't have "sold out", as you put it. If you would be kind enough to point me in the direction of the Misses Brontë, I shall go about my business and leave you to your kiosk.'

Lavender Stamp had received only the briefest of updates from Poppa as he escorted Muddy to the cricket field. She knew that there had been fatalities

195

overnight and that the complexion of the festival had changed, but to what extent she had no idea. The fact that two of the agent's clients were now corpses taking part in a macabre exhibition in the library was certainly beyond her present knowledge. The word 'kiosk' stung more than Penny Stone-Cragg could have imagined, but Lavender decided to err on the side of caution after the bloody nose she'd received the day before.

'If you would care to wait, I'll fetch someone who can help you. As you have observed, I am not able to leave my . . . er . . . KIOSK, or I would be delighted to show you into the festival myself.'

Penny Stone-Cragg was not used to waiting. Ignoring Lavender altogether, she grabbed her briefcase and inhaler from the passenger seat and swung the car door open. Her smart summer trouser suit instantly spoke money and quality, and Lavender knew that she was beaten. The agent ascended the steps to Furcross House and was about to lift the giant knocker when Mr Pushkin opened the door. Glancing at his lanyard and establishing that he was official, she announced herself. 'Penny Stone-Cragg. My clients are appearing at the festival, and I'm here to attend an event or two.'

Mr Pushkin offered his broadest welcome smile. 'I'm sure they'll be delighted to see you. Is it Miss Upstart or Miss Hodge?'

'Neither. I look after Charlene, Emmeline and Ann

196

Brontë,' she clarified, warming to his Russian accent.

The look of horror which replaced the smile was instant. Mr Pushkin shrank back from the agent as if she'd burnt him. 'Ah, one moment please and I will get someone.' He fled down the corridor towards the library, leaving Penny Stone-Cragg to stare at herself in the hatstand mirror and wonder if it was her hot, flushed appearance which had sent the Russian cat away in such haste.

Hettie and Tilly were admiring Morbid's handiwork when Mr Pushkin made his entrance. The panic written right across his face made it very clear that yet another crisis loomed.

'Quick! Someone help! The Brontës' agent – she's just arrived and is asking to speak with them.'

'That could be quite a short conversation unless she's a clairvoyant,' said Hettie. 'Who is she?'

'Miss Penny Stone-Cragg, I think she said.'

'Ooh, she's really famous,' said Tilly. 'I read somewhere that she eats authors for breakfast if she doesn't like them.'

Hettie tried to stay calm. 'Well, maybe we could fob her off with a Butters' pie instead.'

'She'll probably choke on it when she gets a look at this,' Tilly said, not helping by waving her paw at the tableau.

'What shall I do?' demanded Mr Pushkin, verging on a bout of hysteria.

'I'll sort it out. She'll have to know sooner or later, and at least she can have a nice chat with Emmeline. Show her in, and then go and see how Bruiser is. We're not opening this exhibition until after Polly and Nicolette have done their "in conversation with each other" in the events tent. See if he feels up to taking the money on the door. I know he wanted to be involved.'

Mr Pushkin responded well to authority. Pulling himself together, he ushered the agent into the library and beat a hasty retreat through the French windows, leaving Hettie and Tilly to introduce themselves. Mercifully, the display wasn't visible from the library's reception desk, but Hettie knew that she would have to be succinct in giving the background to what the agent was about to see. She offered a blue lanyard by way of a starting point, making it clear that this would give the visitor access to all areas without further challenges, including the hospitality tent. Penny Stone-Cragg eyed up Hettie and Tilly's lanyards, assessing whether red gave them superiority over blue; control was everything, but she decided to let it pass, and – after Hettie had scribbled her name on the tag, forgetting to include the hyphen – she put the lanyard impatiently over her head. Hettie opened her mouth to begin her presentation, but the agent was in no mood for long conversations and wandered across to the display area before anyone could stop her.

The asthma attack lasted longer than usual,

and it was Tilly's quick thinking in grabbing a chair that stopped the agent passing out altogether. The wheezing gradually subsided as the inhaler did its work. Still clutching at her chest, Penny Stone-Cragg finally brought her breathing under control and spoke in short bursts. 'What is . . . the meaning . . . of this? . . . Some sick joke . . . dreamt up . . . by the festival . . . director . . . Under . . . whose instruction . . . were these . . . models made up?'

'Ah,' said Hettie, desperately trying to select her words in the right order. 'The thing is, we've had a situation here overnight, caused entirely by one of your clients running amok. What you see here is a damage limitation measure.'

'Damage limitation? Situation? What on earth are you talking about?' the agent asked, shouting now that her breathing had returned to normal. 'This is the most tasteless, grotesque display of literary culture since Tracy Ermine's bed! Surely Ann Brontë hasn't agreed to be represented in this way? And as for Downton Tabby, is this another of his lurid stunts to make even more money out of a gullible public? And what – or who – may I ask, is the blackened creature at the back supposed to be?'

Hettie cast a look at Tilly, who cast it back. Both cats knew that it was time for some plain speaking. Hettie decided to answer Penny Stone-Cragg's enquiries in the order she had expressed them. 'Ann Brontë had no choice in the matter because she was murdered by her sister in their camper van. That is her actual body. The head and torso you see are also the work of Charlene Brontë, who beheaded Sir Downton last night after his event. The blackened figure in the centre of the display *is* Charlene Brontë, who was struck by lightning whilst trying to murder an operative of mine who was trying to apprehend her. I should also add that, in my opinion, Charlene Brontë would have succeeded in murdering Emmeline Brontë as well had we not intervened at the right moment. The festival was in grave danger of closing prematurely due to your client's actions, and so we decided to offer this tableau as an open and honest statement of what has happened here.'

Hettie was pleased with her truncated version of the situation. Tilly was impressed, and Penny Stone-Cragg was silent, inspecting the display with new eyes. It was some time before she gave any response at all; when it came, it was Hettie who was rendered speechless.

Penny Stone-Cragg rose from her chair and moved closer to the tableau. 'Brilliant! Absolutely brilliant, and I own the rights to two-thirds of it! I knew Charlene would come good in the end, and just think of the book sales! Film rights, a whole load of new territories, and a touring exhibition. Fantastic! Just fantastic! And I still have Emmeline! What joy! She's the only one who could write, anyway. And I'll let her publish all her miserable poetry – it'll sell like hot cakes now that her sisters are victim and murderess. She'll have to update Ann's biography to start with, though – a first-paw account of "Death at the Festival".' The agent had quite forgotten Hettie and Tilly as she paced up and down, talking to herself and brainstorming the lucrative possibilities brought about by the death of two clients. Hettie breathed a sigh of relief. It would appear that the idea of displaying the corpses fitted in perfectly with the ethics of the publishing industry, or rather with the lack of them.

Polly Hodge put paid to the agent's raptures by making her entrance through the French windows. 'Penny, my dear – I wondered if you'd turn out for this festival. Client list getting a bit thin, by the look of things.' She waved a paw at the display. 'I'm writing it up for my next shocker. Far too delicious to ignore, and what fun to be here while it was all going on! A first-paw account and all that – liquid gold for the booksellers.'

Penny Stone-Cragg had always regarded P. D. Hodge as the one that got away and perhaps the biggest mistake she had ever made. When Polly had submitted her first novel, *Cover Her Paws*, Penny had confined it to her slush pile as a book to get round to eventually. Within months, Polly had signed with Flavour and Flavour, quickly becoming their bestselling author and unseating the late Agatha Crispy as the 'Queen of

Crime'. Penny had licked her wounds and tried to avoid noticing Polly's meteoric rise to fame, but the author and her work were ever-present and very hard to ignore.

Now, she prepared her brave face and turned it towards the author. 'I think you'll have to go with an unauthorised account, Polly. Emmeline is in a much better position to write about her sisters, and it's preferable to your turning it into one of your lurid crime fictions – although I'm sure it would be very readable.'

'Maybe we should discuss terms over a festival breakfast?' Polly suggested. 'I'm famished. All these murders work up more than just a literary appetite.'

The idea of breakfast and a nice sit-down was a very attractive prospect, even without the chance to sign up the murder novel of the century from the pen of crime fiction's Goliath. 'That would be lovely,' said the agent, gathering up her briefcase and leading the way to the French windows.

Hettie breathed a sigh of relief. 'Well, I think we got away with that one. Charlene Brontë's rampage has obviously made her agent's day.'

'You were marvellous, though, telling it the way it is,' said Tilly in admiration. 'And the display is magnificent. Morbid has done us proud. What's next?'

'I think I'm going to find a deckchair and sit in the sun,' Hettie said, yawning. 'I'll park myself at the back of the marquee for easy access to the hospitality tent and in case you need any help. What time do your events kick off?'

'I'm putting Polly and Nicolette on at eleven. They've agreed to plug the exhibition, ready for the opening at twelve. I think there'll be a stampede to see it, so we'll need all paws on deck by then. If Bruiser and Mr Pushkin can deal with the tickets and the money, Poppa can be on security. I thought we could let them in by the French windows, then past the display and out through the other door, along the corridor and into the car park at the front. Lavender Stamp can direct them back into the festival through the memorial garden gate, and that way we can keep them moving. I'll ask the Fudges to stand by with first aid in case we get any fainters.'

Hettie was full of admiration for Tilly's plan, mainly because she wasn't involved in it. Her intention for the rest of the day was to snooze in the sun and partake of the Butters' themed meals – but the day still held some surprises, for which neither Hettie nor Tilly had bargained.

CHAPTER FIFTEEN

The hospitality tent was alive with conversation by the time Polly Hodge and Penny Stone-Cragg reached it. They'd picked Nicolette up on the way, as Polly was keen to introduce her to the agent. Had the Brontë sisters not been such a full-time job, Penny would have gladly included Nicolette in her elite stable of authors: her sunny disposition and public persona sold books better than any marketing plan, and she did work hard; youth was also on her side, which is why she was sent to queue for the breakfasts as Polly and the agent made themselves comfortable in the authors' dining area.

'Now, about this book, dear,' Polly began, wasting no time on niceties. 'I can see your point about letting

Emmeline write it, but would it be good enough? That's the real question. I honestly think you need a more mature paw on the typewriter for this one, and the poor girl is in deep shock. It's not the best moment to spring a new project on her, but if you give her time to come to terms with it all, someone else will have snatched the story away. Commission me now and I'll start work on Monday, and Emmeline can write the foreword. How about that?'

Penny Stone-Cragg raised her paw in submission. 'You're absolutely right, and Emmeline isn't the easiest client to work with. God only knows how long it would take her to finish a book like that – she's always writing her bloody poetry. Bonville Brontë had to help her finish *Withering Sights*. She was always getting lost on the moor in bad weather, which meant weeks of convalescence on her chaise longue in the parsonage, scribbling her rhymes instead of applying herself to the fate of Katty and Heatclip. It's a shame he ever started on liquid catnip – he'd have made a very fine writer, certainly better than the painter he became. Anyway, I digress. I'll have the contract drawn up as soon as I get back to Porkshire. At least I'll get to publish one of yours before we both shuffle off to the slush pile in the sky.'

Polly Hodge laughed. It was a refreshing change to have a grown-up conversation with a cat who had been through as much turbulence as she had over the years and was still at the top of her profession.

'How will you manage without Charlene and Ann on your books? A bit of a blow to lose two at once.'

'Well, to be perfectly honest, there were days when I would happily have strangled Charlene myself! She was so aggressive, and Ann just simpered along behind her, lapping up anything she said. Neither of them had much time for Emmeline, although she was born to be a nightmare of a different kind. Out with the fairies doesn't even begin to describe her.'

'You don't seem very shocked by Charlene's murderess escapades. Did you see this coming?'

'No, not at all. There was plenty of sisterly in-fighting, but nothing that suggested fatal consequences. I knew that Charlene hated Downton Tabby, but – to be honest – didn't we all? He was the most obnoxious cat I've ever met. That year I spent as his agent was purgatory. He lived in a completely different world to the rest of us. The arrogance of the upper classes and their complete lack of understanding of the real world defeated me. I had to let him go for my own sanity.'

Nicolette approached with a beaming smile and three all-day breakfasts balanced precariously on a tray. She brought everything to a safe landing and Polly Hodge wasted no time in unloading the plates. The three said very little as they demolished the egg, bacon, sausage and fried bread, and it was Penny Stone-Cragg who eventually broke the silence, addressing her remarks to Nicolette. 'I so enjoyed your *Death of Lucy Cat*. Are there others in the pipeline of a similar nature that I could publish?'

Nicolette swallowed her last piece of fried bread too quickly, getting it stuck in her throat and submitting to a coughing fit which took some time to bring under control. The ever watchful Delirium Treemints came to the rescue with a glass of water and Nicolette gradually regained her composure, her ears turning bright red against her blonde fur. 'I'm promoting my compendium, *London Drains and Other Grimes* at the moment, but I'm halfway through another stand-alone. I have a part-finished rough draft if you'd care to read it?'

Polly Hodge added her support. 'You should take a look at it, Penny dear. It really is very good. I've had a peek myself, and you could have a real hit on your paws.'

'OK, I'm convinced. With your endorsement I clearly have to read it, Polly, although I'll expect a quote from you for the front cover.'

'Of course. That goes without saying.' Polly Hodge rose from the table. 'Come along, Nicolette, my dear – we'd better adjourn to the marquee where our public awaits. Time to sell some books, I think.' The two cats left the agent scribbling in her appointments diary and crossed over to the backstage area of the marquee, where Tilly was waiting to greet them.

The stage was set up with the two chairs which had only recently been occupied by Downton Tabby and Hettie. Nicolette and Polly appeared to rapturous applause and the day's events got underway. They worked well together, and there was a huge respect between them. Polly had mentored Nicolette when she first started to write, and the two cats had become firm friends in spite of their age difference. Polly loved associating with young authors: their enthusiasm and modern perspective on life fuelled her interest in all things, and she, in turn, possessed a self-assured wisdom which she was more than happy to pass on to those who deserved it. The two cats laid out the pros and cons of the crime novel, taking it in turns to discuss each other's books and delighting their audience with some of the more extreme areas of research to which their work had taken them. By the end of their joint presentation, it was clear that murder was an extreme sport for both of them, a challenge to create not just the perfect crime but the nastiest – all in good heart, and in the true tradition of the detective writer.

They took their bows and Nicolette left the stage to slip round to the front of the marquee to greet her fans at her merchandise pop-up. Polly waited for the applause to die down, then addressed the crowd. 'I have been asked to tell you about a couple of changes to the festival running order today. Due to unforeseen circumstances, Downton Tabby's marquee appearance has had to be cancelled.'

The groan of disappointment ran through the audience like a Mexican wave; undaunted, Polly Hodge continued. 'The fact of the matter is that he was murdered by Charlene Brontë last night, as was her sister Ann. Following an act of divine intervention, Charlene is also dead and by way of a bolt of lightning has paid the price for her heinous crimes.'

This time, a collective gasp of horror reverberated around the tent as all eyes were riveted to the cat in the centre of the stage. 'The festival director decided to continue with today's events, as he didn't wish to turn away anyone who had bought a ticket. With this in mind, he has put on a very special display in the library which will be open in a few minutes' time. There will be an extra charge for this display, and I suggest that those of you who are of a nervous disposition give it a miss altogether. You will see the consequences of a true crime in its most lurid detail, and later today Emmeline Brontë – the one surviving sister – will pay tribute to her siblings and their work. On a brighter note, Miss Muddy Fryer will be offering a dance and singing workshop after lunch, and will return to the stage after Emmeline Brontë to give her recital of British murder ballads. The evening will conclude with the folk rock group, Furcross Convention, who will offer a cheerful selection of country dance tunes. Now, would those of you who wish to see the display form an orderly queue outside the French windows to the library?'

Tilly clapped her paws in sheer admiration at Polly's speech. She had been fully expecting a riot over the non-appearance of Downton Tabby; instead, the marquee emptied in seconds and the queue for the library began to snake around the stalls area. She thanked the author and left the tent to check that everything was in place before the library doors were opened, making her way through the memorial garden gate where Lavender Stamp had placed herself ready to direct the crowds back into the festival. Cherry and Hilary Fudge were standing by the main door to Furcross House with their first-aid bags at the ready, and she was pleased to see that Bruiser looked much better; he sat by the French windows with a cash box, ready to take the money. Mr Pushkin was pacing the floor with excitement and Poppa stood by the dais, keen to deter any cats from getting too close to the exhibits. Tilly noticed that Turner Page himself was lurking in the history section, eager to see if the revamped festival would save his bacon *and* the library. Satisfied that all was in place, she nodded to Mr Pushkin, who opened the French windows to several hundred pairs of wide eyes.

CHAPTER SIXTEEN

To say that the festival display had proved to be popular would be a gross understatement. Tilly had calculated that a steady flow of visitors would last for two to three hours at the most, but she hadn't bargained for those cats who would be happy to pay for a second and – in some cases – a third look at the spectacle. Lunchtime came and went and the queue persisted. Muddy Fryer's dance and song workshop was poorly attended but warmly appreciated by the few cats who couldn't stomach the display at all, or who had seen enough the first time round.

The heat of the day was beginning to get to everybody. There had been one or two hissing and spitting sessions in the queue, as well as a certain amount of pushing from cats who were keen to get into the shade of the library. All the stallholders were doing a roaring trade, as those waiting for the display had plenty of time to browse. Jessie had sold out of her decorated wellingtons; Meridian Hambone had had to borrow Turner Page's telephone so that she could place an emergency order for more 'Littertray' T-shirts from Dorcas Ink; and Nicolette Upstart had sold everything she had brought with her and had received several substantial offers for her pop-up stall due to its connection with Downton Tabby's murder.

Betty and Beryl Butter – realising that no one would want to leave the queue to buy the pies and pastries which they'd baked in vast quantities – set up their own trestle table by the re-entry gate in the memorial gardens and hired Bugs Anderton to keep shop. The library display had certainly heightened the appetites of those who emerged from a viewing and Bugs added a sideline of her own, taking advantage of the hot sun by charging three pence for a cup of cold water which she had extracted earlier from the outdoor tap by the potting shed and stored in a large galvanised bucket under the trestle table. The money, she decided, would go to bolster the coffers of the town's Friendship Club, in which she had been the dominant force for years.

Hettie slept through the lunch hour, which was

a rare thing in itself. She awoke to the untrained caterwauling of the cats who had joined Muddy Fryer's singing workshop, and it took her a minute or two to get her bearings; the sleep had been deep and dreamless, and it felt quite strange to be waking up in the memorial gardens at Furcross. Suddenly, the night's events came flooding back to her and bit by bit she reconnected with the present. She glanced across at Bugs Anderton, under siege from those in search of refreshment, and wondered why she was selling pies and pastries. She looked across at the hospitality tent, where Beryl Butter was standing in the entrance, fanning herself with her apron and sharing some happy banter with her sister. Resisting the urge to re-engage too soon, Hettie sat back in her deckchair and enjoyed the sound of Muddy Fryer's voice singing 'The Lark in the Morning'; the song was barely over before Muddy's workshop devotees were having a go themselves, missing the high notes and floundering somewhere in the middle to create a wall of sound which could easily be described as unpleasant. At this point, she needed no further inducements to go and find Tilly. Abandoning her deckchair, she made her way past the workshop and out the other side, where she was met with the pandemonium that had been raging for over two hours.

Tilly was stationed at the French windows to the

library as the queue jostled and arched like one of Terry Scratchit's monsters. Hettie noticed that the bookstall had been cleaned out of all Downton Tabby and Brontë books, gobbled up as fast as the Butters' pies.

She pushed through the crowds until she reached Tilly's side. 'How's it all going?' she asked. 'I thought they'd all be through by now.'

'So did I,' Tilly replied, straightening the bandana which had slipped down over one eye. 'The trouble is they're all going round again. I was just wondering what to do about it.'

Hettie looked back along the queue. 'I think we'll have to start directing them into the events marquee from the memorial garden gate. Emmeline Brontë will be on after Muddy has finished her workshop, and they'll all want to see her. Lavender Stamp and Bugs Anderton are stationed by the gate so I'll go and tell them to put a stop on the returnees. Lavender will love to be given some extra authority. You know her – any opportunity for a spot of caustic bullying, and that's exactly what's needed to sort this queue out.'

Tilly was more grateful than she could say: she was hot, tired out, and in need of a very long sleep. 'If you could cover for me, I'll go and get a nice cold drink and sit out of the sun for a bit. I'll have to sort Emmeline out soon, and I ought to let her know that her agent has turned up. I'll speak to Lavender and Bugs on my way through.'

Leaving Hettie to martial the front of the queue, Tilly fought her way back to the events marquee where Muddy Fryer was engaged in an energetic bout of step dancing, much to the delight of her fans. Even Polly Hodge was pointing her toes at the back of the tent, and Jessie had taken time out from her stall to come and watch; now that the wellingtons had all been snapped up, she'd decided to enjoy the festival for herself. Seeing Tilly, she crossed over to her. 'You look all in. Shall we go and have a sit-down?'

Tilly appreciated Jessie's concern and the two cats made their way to the hospitality tent and out of the day's ferocious heat. The tent was cool and peaceful. Delirium Treemints had nodded off behind her samovar and the Butters were taking a break and doing a crossword, with Betty reading out the clues as Beryl solved them. The Crime Teas had been laid out on plates, ready to take through to the marquee; the freshly baked scones were piled high with cream and jam, and Beryl had stuck a small plastic dagger in the top of each one, dipped in strawberry jam for full effect. The wheelbarrow that had so recently been used for transporting bodies had been requisitioned, scrubbed and made ready to ferry the food across the memorial gardens. Betty looked up from her clues as Tilly and Jessie entered the tent. 'You two look like you could do with a treat. Help yourselves to a Crime Tea while you can.'

Tilly slumped down at the nearest table while Jessie responded to Betty's invitation and collected a plate of scones and two ice-cold bottles of ginger beer from the counter. Tilly stared at the scones, wondering if she would ever be hungry again. Her nose and ears were burnt from the sun, her thick long fur felt like it was suffocating her, and her body was wracked with pain from her arthritis.

'Come on,' Jessie coaxed. 'Get one of these scones down you. You need to keep your strength up.'

'I haven't got any strength left,' Tilly said, reaching for the ginger beer. 'I just want to go to sleep for a hundred years.'

'No point in that – just think what you'd miss. Why don't you have a nap now? Emmeline isn't on until after tea, so you won't be needed until then. I can cover for you if anything comes up.'

Tilly hugged her friend with the little strength she had left, downed the ginger beer and hiccuped her way to a deckchair which someone had dragged into the tent. She had just closed her eyes for a second when Penny Stone-Cragg shattered the peace. 'Ah, there you are. I've been informed that you are in charge of artists and I think I should speak with Emmeline before her event. I gather she's resting. Perhaps you could take me to her?'

Before Tilly could reply, Jessie intervened. 'I'm happy to show you to the accommodation block. Miss Tilly's on a break just now and I'm taking over for a bit.'

The agent looked Jessie up and down, deemed her to be reliable and followed her out of the tent, leaving Tilly to her much-needed sleep. Jessie led her across the memorial gardens, taking care to avoid the deep puddles that still persisted after the storm. The sun had dried the ground out, but – where the graves were sited – the overnight rain had settled in miniature lakes, several inches deep and several feet across. The agent tottered on her heels, hanging on to Jessie's paw as she steered her through the obstacle course and arriving at the accommodation block a little out of breath.

The two cats entered the hallway and Jessie stared at the doors that confronted them, having forgotten to ask Tilly which room Emmeline Brontë was occupying. She employed a process of elimination, knocking on each one in turn; the first two brought no response, but the third was opened by a sleepy Darius Bonnet. Penny Stone-Cragg recognised him immediately. 'Darius, my dear boy – I had no idea you were still with Downton Tabby. I thought you'd have had enough years ago. Bad luck all this business, though. If you need a job, give me a ring. My garden in Porkshire needs a strong pair of paws and it would be nice to be driven about occasionally.'

Darius blinked through swollen eyes. The tears he had shed for his master had all dried up, but his heart was still aching. Since Downton Tabby took him on, he had responded to every hour of his benefactor's life, sharing his secrets, serving him in everything, and enjoying the lifestyle which success had delivered. Their servant–master relationship had been one of absolute trust and loyalty, and the fact that Darius had been absent when Downton Tabby had needed him most was preying heavily on his mind.

'That's a very kind offer,' he said, trying to hide his dishevelled appearance behind the door, 'but I've no idea what I'm going to do next. My responsibility now is to return Sir Downton to his ancestral home for a decent burial. After that, I think I'll see which way the wind blows.'

'I completely understand,' said the agent, trying to be sympathetic. 'You know where I am. Could you point us to Emmeline Brontë's room?'

'Next door but one,' said Darius, ending the conversation by closing the door and leaving them to follow his directions.

'Emmeline, dear,' said Penny Stone-Cragg as she tapped on the door. 'It's Penny here – will you let me in?'

There was no immediate response, but a shuffling from inside the room saved the agent from knocking again. The door opened and Jessie turned on her heel, leaving the two to their conversation. When she emerged back into the sunlight, she noticed that the monstrous queue had finally died down and the events marquee was now filling up with cats, all keen for a Crime Tea and a good seat for the surviving Brontë's performance.

CHAPTER SEVENTEEN

What passed between agent and client will never truly be known. There were no witnesses to Penny Stone-Cragg's fatal asthma attack, although she may have survived had she not fallen face down in one of the deeper puddles in the memorial garden. Emmeline was first on the scene and had seemingly done her best to offer assistance to the dying cat, but the Brontë sister was no first-aider and panic had taken over, resulting in vital minutes being lost. Polly Hodge – on her way across for tea – gave the alarm and Hilary and Cherry Fudge were called, but no amount of textbook resuscitation could bring the agent back.

Emmeline stood by, wringing her paws as the agent's

death was confirmed by Cherry, who established that there was no pulse and no breath on the compact mirror that she always carried in case a relevant situation arose.

'What am I to do?' Emmeline cried, finding her voice. 'I have no one left. My sisters are murdered and my agent is dead. I have nothing but the moor to comfort me. This is my darkest of hours.'

Hettie was summoned by Polly Hodge and arrived on the scene in time to witness the strange form of Greek tragedy which was being played out. Emmeline Brontë, still in her nightdress, sat in a puddle cradling her dead agent's head and wailing.

Tilly, awoken by the noise, stumbled out of the hospitality tent rubbing her eyes and joined Hettie for a ringside seat. 'Poor Emmeline,' she said, taking in the situation. 'She's had a non-stop run of bad luck. I thought Penny Stone-Cragg was going to keel over earlier in front of the display. She wasn't well when she arrived, and, with all this heat, I suppose it was always going to end like this.'

'Somebody had better sort Emmeline out,' Hettie muttered, a little unsympathetically. 'She's got to pull herself together. She's on in half an hour, and agent or no agent the show must go on.'

Cherry and Hilary Fudge gently brought Emmeline to her feet, leaving the dead cat in the puddle which had drowned her. Together, they escorted the author back to her room, where they bathed her and assisted her into her stage clothes.

'Looks like we've another one for the Brontë's camper van,' said Hettie. 'We may as well put the body in there. I expect Emmeline might be happy to drive it back to Porkshire in the morning, along with her two sisters. Without Penny Stone-Cragg, there's no chance that the exhibition will travel, and the best place for them is in that godforsaken graveyard above Teethly.'

'What about Downton Tabby?' asked Tilly.

'Well, I think we can leave him to Darius. We don't want the festival involved in funeral costs.'

Poppa strode across the memorial garden to report that the display was now closed and that Bruiser and Mr Pushkin were busily counting the proceeds. 'Turned out to be a brilliant earner,' he said, assisting Hettie with the agent's body. 'Where's this one going?'

'Put her in the Brontës' camper for now. We're keeping this one quiet. It makes a change to have a natural death round here, but it's a bit of bad luck all the same.'

Tilly went ahead to open the garden gate and the camper's back doors as Hettie and Poppa struggled in a somewhat ungainly manner with the dead cat, leaving the body on one of the lower bunks. Poppa returned to the marquee to check the stage arrangements for Emmeline's appearance, and Hettie and Tilly retired to hospitality for a quick cup of tea. Emmeline Brontë's wailing had woken Delirium Treemints from her slumbers and she was now wielding a giant tea pot, correctly anticipating that after yet another fatality there would be a rush on hot, sugary drinks. Polly Hodge and Nicolette Upstart sat consoling each other on the deals that had died in the memorial garden puddle, promising to work on the Furcross festival murder book together. There was no doubt that it would be a bestseller, and being able to include the death of a literary agent was, as Polly put it, 'the icing on the cake, dear.'

Hettie and Tilly gratefully received their tea. A lot of it had been slopped in the saucers, as Delirium's nerves had returned to haunt her with the news of another death. She had recently become apprentice to the town's psychical practitioner Irene Peggledrip and was now convinced that the dead returned to confuse the living – especially if you dressed in purple and bathed yourself in candlelight. Delirium was still a novice, but she knew enough to understand that violent death bred malevolent spirits, which is why she had kept herself well away from the macabre display in the library and concentrated solely on dispensing beverages.

'It's a real shame about Penny Stone-Cragg,' said Tilly, licking the cream off one of Beryl's scones. 'I thought she was an interesting sort of cat – clever, really. I wonder what Emmeline will do now?'

'Laugh all the way to the bank if I was her. Just think – no more agent's fees, all those royalties from her dead sisters' books, and a bestseller of her own. And when word gets out about all that's happened here, the book sales will go through the roof. She'll be able to buy her bloody moor and the rest of Porkshire as well.'

Tilly giggled at Hettie's unsympathetic view of the situation. 'I suppose I'd better go across and escort her to the stage. I'll be glad when this event is over and we're on the home run.' Hettie had to agree, and the two friends parted company in the memorial gardens, Tilly in search of the remaining Brontë and Hettie to the backstage area to bag a good vantage point for the spectacle which was about to begin.

Emmeline Brontë set sail from the accommodation block and glided serenely towards the stage, looking every bit the tragic spirit of her beloved moor. Tilly had been relieved and pleasantly surprised by how cleverly the Fudges had transformed the mud- and tear-stained cat into a magnificent vision of gothic beauty, as if she had stepped out of her own book. She was the manifestation of Katty Earnshaw as she mounted the stage to thunderous applause. Every cat on the festival site was there, and even the Butter sisters had taken their aprons off to lurk at the back of the marquee. Delirium Treemints wheeled her tea trolley across to stand on it so she could get a good view, and Bugs

Anderton and Lavender Stamp flaunted their staff lanyards to secure positions right at the front of the stage.

Tilly held her breath as Emmeline stood motionless in the middle of the platform, willing her to say something. The applause had been replaced by absolute silence, and the audience waited. Eventually, as if woken from a trance, Emmeline lifted her head and stared out across the sea of expectant cats. With tears in her eyes, she began:

High waving heather, 'neath stormy blasts bending,
Moonlight and midnight and bright shiny stars;
Roaring like thunder, like soft music sighing,
Shadows on shadows advancing and flying.
Changing forever from midnight to noon,
Coming as swiftly and fading as soon.

Hettie yawned and wondered how long the poem was likely to last, when suddenly it stopped, without any warning. The audience was caught out as well, and it was a few seconds before a nervous smattering of applause developed into full-blown appreciation. Emmeline waited for everyone to settle, sitting down in the chair that Poppa had placed in the middle of the stage.

'Today was going to be a celebration of my work,' she began, 'but now I find myself in such grief that it is no celebration at all. I would like to think badly of my sister Charlene for what she has done in this place, but I cannot. She has been a guiding light to my sister Ann and me, and in all honesty I cannot contemplate a life without her.

'Instead of talking about my own book, I thought I would tell you about my family. As you know, we come from Porkshire and live up on the moors above Teethly, where the chimney smoke is black and life is short. My mother, who is long dead, was born in Cornwall. My grandmother was in service there, and got herself in trouble with the master's son. She was allowed to keep her kitten, but she was sent away to work at Teethly Grange, a big house in Porkshire, where she raised my mother and married her off to the local vicar, my father. My grandmother was sweet on one of the servants in the big house and she married him, but he died of blood poisoning after having his paws chopped off.'

There was a groan of distaste from the audience as Emmeline warmed to her subject, and Hettie and Tilly sat bolt upright. 'When my grandmother was too old to serve, she was turned out and died in Teethly Workhouse. My sisters and I never knew her, as we were very small kittens when she died. My mother was broken-hearted when she found out that her mother had ended her days in such a terrible place, and she vowed to revenge her passing with those at the big house – but she died before she could do anything.

There was a bad outbreak of ginger beer lung disease, and lots of cats died that winter. After she passed, father decided to move us out of Teethly for our health and up onto the moor, where his ancestors' house had come up for sale. That's where we live now.

'My beloved brother, Bonville, made friends with one of the cats at Teethly Grange, who led him into all sorts of trouble gambling and fighting, and eventually he developed a dependency for liquid catnip. For months and months I sat by his bed as he went slowly out of his mind, occasionally coming back to us long enough to suck on a cheese triangle. He was a scholar and a fine painter, and now he lies in the churchyard along with the rest of my family, all of whom have perished at the paws of Downton Tabby and his vile family!'

The audience gasped as one, but Emmeline continued. 'You may all shrink back at my words, but I tell you this – Downton Tabby deserved to die. He made promises to recompense us for our loss and then ridiculed us in public. He was planning to film his next TV series at the big house on our doorstep, featuring our brother and my grandmother as characters. He even asked my sister Ann to play the part of the tweenie who died in front of a fireplace and had to be cleared away! I am the last voice, and I will not mourn the passing of such an evil cat who has destroyed my family in so many ways.'

Hettie looked into the audience, where cats were becoming very agitated. The grace and serenity had fallen from Emmeline, to be replaced by a steely, threatening attitude which seemed dangerous. It was Bugs Anderton who took the heat out of the situation. 'Miss Brontë – please may we hear more of your beautiful poetry?'

Emmeline stared down at Bugs, and for a moment Hettie thought that she might lash out at her, but she gained control and stood up as silence once again descended on the marquee:

Cold in the earth—and snow piled above thee,
Far, far removed, cold in the dreary grave!
Cold in the earth—and fourteen wild Decembers,
Faithful, indeed, is the spirit that remembers
After such years of change and suffering!

Without even waiting for the applause, Emmeline Brontë turned and descended the steps at the back of the stage, then swept out of the marquee and was gone before anyone could even thank her.

'Do you think I should go after her?' asked Tilly, as the audience began to express its annoyance with a slow clapping of paws.

'No. I should leave her alone for a bit – she's in no mood for sympathy. This crowd has been short-changed, so we need to get Muddy on as soon as we can. What

231

time are the Butters serving their Deadly Dinners?'

'We agreed seven, but I could ask them to bring things forward.'

Hettie looked for Muddy Fryer in the crowd and located her perched on the festival bar at the back of the marquee. 'I'll sort Muddy out while you go and arrange the dinners. We need to distract this lot before things turn nasty. I expect there are a lot of Downton Tabby fans who are pretty hacked off out there.'

'Just like his head, then,' murmured Tilly, more to herself than to anyone else.

CHAPTER EIGHTEEN

At Tilly's request, the Butter sisters rose to the challenge of bringing their Deadly Dinners forward. Muddy, like the trouper she was, wasted no time in enthralling the audience with a selection of rousing Jacobite songs while they waited for the food to arrive.

Leaving Poppa in charge of the stage, Hettie made her way back to the hospitality tent where she found Tilly and Bugs Anderton in deep conversation. She sat down with them and listened as Bugs waved a small book of Emmeline Brontë's poetry in the air.

'I know them off by heart. I bought this from the gift shop in Teethly last summer. Emmeline had had them printed up herself, and I was hoping she might sign it for me.'

'But what are you saying?' demanded Tilly, looking bewildered.

'I'm saying that it's "midnight and moonlight", and "the stars are shining" and not "shiny". The rest of it was just a few lines in no particular order, and the end bit was completely wrong: it's fifteen wild Decembers, not fourteen.'

Hettie could see that Bugs had got herself into a bit of a state, which was the last thing that she or Tilly needed. Calling on another distraction tactic, she suggested that Bugs should visit Darius Bonnet and invite him to supper. As far as Hettie was concerned, anything was better than discussing the finer points – if there were any – of Emmeline Brontë's poetry, and anyway she wanted to talk to Tilly about the revelations that had emerged during the author's short but illuminating event.

Bugs shuffled off with her poetry book in the direction of the accommodation block, leaving Hettie and Tilly to chew over Emmeline's words and the two large home-made beef burgers which Betty had banged down in front of them. Resisting the thick red chilli sauce that was clearly the deadly bit, the two friends chewed and licked their way through the meat, agreeing that they were the best Deadly Dinners they'd ever had. Hettie leant back in her chair.

'At least we know now why Charlene Brontë hated Downton Tabby enough to kill him. He stupidly goaded her by wallowing in the stories that affected her own family in front of a packed audience. And that newspaper cutting you found about the filming in Teethly – maybe the Brontës intended to confront him about it. There was a bit of a spat going on before he did his event.'

'But what about poor Ann?' said Tilly. 'Why did Charlene kill her? And she tried to kill Emmeline, too. If it hadn't been for Bruiser, all three sisters would be dead.'

'I think we'll have to have another chat with Emmeline,' said Hettie, getting to her feet. 'You have a rest and I'll go and sort a few things out. We need to take the display down and load Charlene and flat-packed Ann into the camper. I assume that Darius will be happy to find space in the Rolls-Royce for Downton Tabby. Quite frankly, I'll be happy to have all the corpses and their entourages heading homeward as soon as possible so we can all get back to normal – whatever that is.'

Tilly scrambled back into her deckchair and was asleep in seconds. Hettie passed through the marquee, where hundreds of cats were enjoying their Deadly Dinners. The Butters had done the festival proud, and the ghoulish vat of hot red chilli was proving a real hit with those who enjoyed living dangerously. Hettie nodded to Poppa, who was busy setting up Turner Page's drum kit for the final set from Furcross

235

Convention which would close the festival.

'I think we should shift the display while everyone's busy with the food,' she said.

Poppa put the cymbals in place and followed her out of the marquee, picking up the wheelbarrow on the way. The library was peaceful, and Mr Pushkin and Turner Page sat together at the desk, enjoying their supper and sharing the occasional grunt of appreciation.

Hettie and Poppa sized up the job. 'Let's get Charlene down first,' Hettie suggested. 'Muddy will be pleased to get her broadsword back, and I'll be pleased to get this burnt offering into the camper.'

'What about the eyes?'

'Let's leave them the way they are. Emmeline has tried to paint her sister as some sort of superhero, and with laser eyes she looks the part.'

They struggled with the blackened corpse and eventually got it into the wheelbarrow. Avoiding the crowds, they wheeled the body out through the front entrance and round to the camper. Leaving Charlene Brontë on the bottom bunk opposite her agent, the two cats returned for Ann, who gave them very little trouble. They put her back on the top bunk, where her sister had suffocated her, and closed the back doors of the camper, which had now become a rather gruesome mausoleum.

'I'll go and get the keys to the Roller,' said Poppa,

letting himself into the accommodation block. He returned seconds later with Darius Bonnet and Bugs Anderton, who were about to go to supper. Darius looked upset and handed Poppa the keys.

'There's a blanket in the boot. If you could wrap him in it and put him on the back seat, I'd be really grateful.' Poppa nodded and followed Hettie back to the library, where they reunited Downton Tabby with his head and placed him in the comfort of his own Rolls-Royce.

When they returned to the library, Mr Pushkin and Turner Page had already removed the dais and folded the purple curtain up, pleased to have the library free of bodies and elated by the three buckets full of money which sat waiting to be banked behind the library desk. Mr Pushkin took great care in locking the doors, and the four cats strode across the stalls area towards the marquee, where Muddy Fryer was about to give her final performance of the day.

Hettie stared at the sea of satisfied cats. The sun had finally given up and sunk into the west, leaving a trail of blood-red sky which made everything glow in a strange ethereal light. To everyone's relief, the heat was finally dying down, along with the tensions that had been present throughout the day. Hettie had played some pretty strange festivals during her music days, but this one would always stand out, not just for the body count but for the community spirit that had transformed a total disaster into a miracle of success. She glanced across at the happy band of helpers who now huddled together in the backstage area of the marquee, enjoying Muddy's opening song. Hilary and Cherry Fudge, the mother and daughter first-aiders who had most probably saved Bruiser's life, even if they had failed to resuscitate the Brontës' agent; Poppa, who had started the festival in charge of car parking and ended up as stage security and corpse removal; Polly Hodge, the voice of reason during the darkest hour of the night; Nicolette Upstart and her unshakable sunny disposition, even when her pop-up merch tent was stained with tragedy. And then there were the harridans of the town: Lavender Stamp and Bugs Anderton, difficult cats at the best of times but stepping up to the plate when most needed and a perfect contrast to the shy, nervous Delirium Treemints, whose constant flow of hot drinks had thrown a lifeline into a troubled sea of despond. It was no surprise to Hettie that her landladies, the redoubtable Butter sisters, had done their bit, but she had to admire the way in which they had completely disconnected themselves from the horror that unfolded, bringing a much-needed normality to the hospitality tent as they banged about in their field kitchen, creating plate upon plate of delicious food for the whole of the festival site. Choosing a hero among so many would prove an impossible task, Hettie thought, but Bruiser would be top of her list for medals: he had offered his life to protect Emmeline Brontë from her sister, and he now sat at the side of the stage swathed in bandages, tapping the only paw that didn't hurt to Muddy's music. And Muddy herself had been an absolute trouper, using her remarkable voice to calm the restless and frightened spirits of her fellow performers and mesmerising her audience as only she could.

Hettie looked for Tilly and as if by magic she appeared through the tent flap, sleepy-eyed and a little ruffled. Tilly had been one of the festival's stars, too. She had been working for months to make it a success and had picked up and run with every disaster that had been hurled at her, including – and especially – the Brontës, who had been trouble from the moment they'd arrived. Hettie allowed herself a moment of pride and satisfaction for the contribution that her No. 2 Feline Detective Agency had made. It had been created on a whim and was now, it seemed, a force to be reckoned with, carrying enough clout to involve many of the town's notables in times of crisis.

Hettie stood next to Tilly as Muddy stormed through an exhilarating set of murder ballads, delighting her audience with tales of wicked witches, malevolent ghosts and dead damsels. She was joined occasionally on stage by a member of Furcross Convention, who added a concertina here and a violin there, depending on what the song required. The end of her set came too soon for the audience, and they clapped and stomped for four encores before letting the singer leave the stage to a standing ovation. Muddy was delighted with her reception, even more so when Poppa reunited her with her broadsword, so recently wrenched from the paws of Charlene Brontë; she held the sword aloft with joy before heading to the bar for a flagon of festival ale to celebrate its safe return.

Hettie signalled to Tilly and the two cats left the noise of the marquee behind for the peace of the memorial gardens. 'I think we should try and have a chat with Emmeline,' Hettie said. 'We've loaded her camper with the bodies, and she's in for a bit of a strange journey back to Porkshire with that lot in the back.'

'I haven't seen her since she ran from the stage, but I suppose she's back in her room. We could go and see if she'd like some supper as an excuse to talk to her.'

CHAPTER NINETEEN

Charlene Brontë had just finished packing her sisters' suitcases when Hettie and Tilly arrived at her door. She knew they would come and she was expecting them. The pretence of being her mild-mannered sister was over. Her attempt at Emmeline's pathetic, doom-laden poetry had almost given her away and she was no longer in the mood to play games. Penny Stone-Cragg had pushed her luck by threatening to expose the lie and had been the easiest of her victims, but the two cats from the detective agency were a little more problematic. To wipe the slate clean, she needed to strike them down and leave before any more cats became suspicious. She would give herself enough time to confess and allow them to appreciate the brilliance of her actions, but dead cats told no tales and leaving their bodies to rot on the Porkshire moors would be her personal homage to her sister Emmeline. Adding a couple more corpses to the camper would be of little consequence, and the town would care very little for two missing detectives when the news of Downton Tabby's murder hit the newspaper stands. Charlene prepared the ropes and put the knife where she could pick it up easily. She was ready and waiting.

When Hettie and Tilly reached the accommodation block, Darius Bonnet was just leaving. He'd packed the luggage into the back of the Rolls-Royce and was about to say his farewells to Bugs Anderton, to whom he had clearly taken a shine. Having made arrangements to meet up soon, Bugs stood in the car park ready to wave him off.

As the Rolls-Royce made slow progress towards the gates of Furcross, it occurred to Hettie that life would be very different now for Darius – a servant who had enjoyed the status of friend and confidant, suddenly reduced to nothing. She mused over whether he would have to hand over the Rolls-Royce with Downton Tabby's body on his return to Sir Downton's ancestral home. Would he be turned out and disposed of like past retainers had been? And which of the fat aristocats would inherit the vast fortune that his master had accumulated? The death of a celebrity brought its own questions, and loyalty meant nothing in the scheme of things.

Bugs nodded to them as she walked back to the hospitality tent, too distraught to speak. She hated goodbyes, and needed a cup of Delirium's hot, sweet tea to comfort her. Hettie and Tilly made their way down the corridor to Emmeline's room, where Tilly knocked discreetly in case the author was asleep. But the cat who flung the door open was very wide awake. She pulled the two friends into her room and shut the door firmly behind them. 'How nice of you both to drop in,' she said, circling around them. 'Please take a seat.'

She pushed Tilly roughly onto the bed and Hettie froze, long enough for their adversary to pick up the knife. 'Ah, I see you're a little surprised by your welcome. Sit next to your friend and we'll have a little chat.' The cat pointed the knife at Hettie's chest, gently pushing her towards the bed. 'Before we begin, I think it best if we make you both a little more comfortable. We don't want you making a dash for the door, do we?' She picked up the ropes and threw them at Hettie and Tilly. 'I want you to tie your legs up nice and tight, leaving a good bit of rope for me to finish the job.'

Hettie glared back at her. 'Why are you doing this? We saved your life! We stopped your sister from murdering you.'

The demented Brontë threw her head back and cackled. 'You must be so stupid to think you could outsmart me! You don't even know who you're talking to. Just get those ropes on and I'll introduce myself.'

Tilly responded first by tying the rope around her legs; Hettie followed more slowly, keeping a watchful eye on the knife-waving cat in front of them. When their legs were secured, their new-found enemy put the knife down long enough to bind their paws, making escape impossible. 'Now then,' she said, retrieving the knife and teasing Tilly's whiskers with it, 'I am *Charlene* Brontë. She is not the blackened creature you've paraded in front of the hordes of cats who have passed through the library. That was my pathetic little sister, Emmeline, who has got in my way since the day she was born. And as for my dear sister Ann, her existence was pointless. She couldn't stomach Downton Tabby's death. After I'd sliced his head off, she ran to Emmeline telling tales, so I did her a favour and silenced her – but not before I'd made her put up that nice little display on the bookstall.'

Charlene Brontë shifted the knife towards Hettie and then back to Tilly, as if conducting an orchestra. 'It will come as no surprise to you that I am going to kill you both. I shall slit your throats, I think – that would be a most pleasing way to end the day. You must decide between you who goes first and who watches, but before I get to work you must have so many questions to ask. Isn't that why you are here?'

Tilly tried very hard to suppress the sob which rose in her throat. Hettie stared straight ahead, struck dumb by the sudden realisation of her own stupidity. The swapping of the lanyards, the marked resemblance between the three sisters – it had all been an elaborate game, played out with masterly precision. Charlene Brontë had been magnificent and was still in total control. She tried to think back to when the deception started and voiced her thoughts. 'If Emmeline was the one struck down by lightning, why was she trying to kill our friend Bruiser?'

Charlene smiled, showing a row of perfectly sharp white teeth. 'Because I told her he was going to kill her. She was only defending herself. He arrived just in time, actually. I thought I was going to have to get rid of her myself, but fate intervened and you swallowed the lie, hook, line, and sinker. It was so easy to become Emmeline after that, lapping up all the sympathy and being the only survivor of her wicked, murderous sister Charlene.'

'And what about Penny Stone-Cragg? Did she recognise you?'

'Of course she did,' admitted Charlene, warming to her subject. 'She arrived at my door wheezing, and all I had to do was make things worse for her. I confessed my sins and then sat on her inhaler. It was great fun watching her gasp for breath. How she found the strength to escape, I'll never know, but the puddle finished her, much to my relief – and hers, no doubt. I never liked her. She always preferred

Emmeline and Ann, and she didn't like the way I ran things. She was always interfering. Once she even suggested that I rewrote *Jane Hair* to make it more like *Withering Sights* because Emmeline's book was much more believable. I laughed in her face – lacy mittens, tortured landscapes and ghosts! What sort of book is that?'

Tilly, who'd recovered herself, was tempted to say 'a very good one' but she kept silent.

'It's amusing to think that you accepted me as Emmeline so easily,' Charlene continued, pointing the knife back at Tilly. 'When you came to my door, I had only just changed out of my bloody clothes and finished sedating dear Emmeline and tying her to the bed. I have to admit, I was quite shocked later to find that she'd escaped. It was then that the storm played into my paws. I went to find her, and she was cowering under the bookstall with the sword. I convinced her that we were being hunted and she lashed out at anyone who came near. The bolt of lightning was a stroke of luck for me as well as for your injured friend – it meant that I could become Emmeline, leaving you all to assume that that blackened piece of toast was me, Charlene Brontë, the murderer. I suppose in the end you were right about that.'

The knife moved back to Hettie, who responded by asking a question. 'Why did you bother holding

Emmeline captive? Surely it would have been easier to kill her as well.'

'I was going to kill her. In fact, I was going to slit her wrists with this knife to make it look as if she'd killed herself out of remorse – it's the sort of thing she would have done. But thanks to your interference, events overtook me. Your little friend here disturbed her in our room and threw me into a bit of a panic, but it all turned out quite nicely in the end.'

'So the cat who frightened me in your room was Emmeline?' asked Tilly, feeling braver.

Charlene laughed again. 'I think she would have been much more frightened of you at that point. She must have been climbing the walls with fear, because she hated storms. She always hid under the stairs at the slightest puff of Porkshire wind.'

Hettie watched as Charlene forced the knife into Tilly's face, trying to come up with another question that might delay the inevitable. 'What do you plan to do next? I mean after you've killed us. Surely returning to Porkshire will be a bit difficult after everything that's happened here?'

'Oh, I shall not stay long in that godforsaken place. Once I have disposed of the bodies on the moor, I shall put my father out of his misery, lock up the house and walk away. As Emmeline Brontë, I shall be a very rich cat indeed, and I shall buy a house where the sun always shines and leave those dark, forbidding winters

247

behind me. I will even publish her awful poems as my own and enjoy every penny that comes from them. I have lived a pitiful life, perched above the black mills of Teethly, sharing all I have with my sisters in that claustrophobic house on the edge of the moor, and with only the latest burial in the graveyard to brighten my day. My father has served his time on this earth. He mourns my mother in the twilight world in which he now exists, and he will be pleased to join her in the heaven he has spent his life promoting.'

The knock on the door made Charlene jump and she inadvertently stabbed Tilly in the cheek with the knife. Hettie swung her legs high into the air, knocking Charlene Brontë to the ground. The knife spun out of her paw and shot across the floor as Hettie hauled herself off the bed and landed with all her weight on top of the angry cat. Tilly, half blinded by the blood that spurted from her face, bounced across the room to the door and turned the key in the lock with her teeth, allowing Poppa to burst into the room.

'Blimey!' was all he could say as he took in the scene. He wasted no time in retrieving the knife from the floor and sliced through the rope that bound Tilly, allowing her to mop her cheek with her bandana. Then he moved to free Hettie as Charlene Brontë rolled away from her, hissing and spitting, her claws arched like talons, daring any of them to come near her. With one mighty leap, she vaulted through the open door, down the hallway and out into the night. Seconds later, Poppa gave chase with Hettie and Tilly limping along behind – but they were all too late.

The camper's engine sprang into life as Charlene pushed her foot down hard on the accelerator. The van lurched and resisted until she released the handbrake, then shot forward suddenly, missing the gates entirely and hurling itself at the wall with an almighty bang. Hettie, Tilly and Poppa stared in silence at what remained of the vehicle as it hissed and poured its lifeblood all over the driveway. A mixture of petrol, oil and water gushed from the mangled wreck, filling the air with an acrid smoke. The three cats waited at a safe distance to see if the van would catch fire. Hettie, shocked by the spectacle before her, gradually began to take in the carnage: the bodies that had been so carefully placed in the back of the camper lay strewn across the wreckage: Penny Stone-Cragg had come to rest on a burning tyre; Emmeline's charred remains had fragmented and popped up at various locations within the crash site; and flat-packed Ann had been catapulted into Mr Pushkin's prized tea roses. But there was no sign of Charlene.

Suddenly, the whole scene ignited into a giant wall of flames. A series of small explosions followed, and the friends stood back from the heat as the flames – fuelled by petrol – became a raging inferno. Hettie shielded her eyes from the intensity of light as a small fireball detached itself from the main event, rolling along the ground towards the gates and screaming with such intensity that Tilly was forced to put her paws over her ears.

'Oh my God!' shouted Hettie. 'It's Charlene – she's survived the crash, only to be burnt alive.'

'Just like the mad cat in the attic,' Poppa said as the fireball burnt itself out, leaving a pile of blackened ashes at the gates to Furcross House.

The town's part-time fire brigade was swift in its response to Mr Pushkin's emergency phone call, and within minutes of its arrival, the driveway and car park were covered with fluffy white foam as a precaution against any further explosions. As a reward for their labours, the firecats were served with a Deadly Dinner each, which they ate on the steps of Furcross House, keeping a keen eye on the crash site – now a surreal, snowy landscape, as Tilly excitedly pointed out.

Furcross Convention had been encouraged to keep the festivalgoers entertained until the emergency was over, and now – an hour later than planned – a mass exodus of cats flooded through the gates and out into Sheba Gardens, having no real idea of the carnage that lay beneath the blanket of foam through which they paddled. The intensity of the fire had consumed everything, including Mr Pushkin's rose garden, Penny Stone-Cragg's Morris convertible, and Lavender Stamp's ticket kiosk. Days later, when the clear-up began, only the mangled wreck of the camper van was left to bear witness to Charlene Brontë's reign of terror, although the black scars of the cremations remained until Turner Page ordered several tons of gravel from Agricat and Co.

After a heartfelt vote of thanks from Turner Page for what he called 'the outstanding service provided by the No. 2 Feline Detective Agency', Hettie and Tilly bade farewell to the bedraggled company and left Furcross House. They fell wearily into Mr Tiddles' taxi, accompanied by the Butter sisters and Bruiser, all bound for the same address. Hettie reflected on how she'd almost forgotten what their small but very comfortable room looked like, although her comments fell on deaf ears: all but Sterling Tiddles himself had fallen asleep for the short journey home. No dreams or nightmares visited the occupants of the high street bakery that night; just a long, deep sleep which endured well into the middle of Sunday morning, when the house awoke to the sound of the newspaper clattering through the letter box.

CHAPTER TWENTY

Betty and Beryl Butter had decided over their late morning tea that they would put on a 'survivors' tea party' in their back garden that afternoon. All the helpers from the festival were to be invited, and no expense spared. By the time the glad tidings reached Hettie and Tilly's room, nearly all the guests had been asked. Beryl had spent a considerable amount of time on the phone, while her sister invaded the ovens with tin upon tin of cake mixture, followed by row upon row of sausage rolls and cheese straws.

'I'm not being difficult,' said Hettie, being difficult, 'but I've just spent two bloody days of my life with that lot, and now we've got to spend the whole of Sunday afternoon with them as well.' Tilly giggled and braced herself for the rant that was about to follow. 'To say it's been a nightmare just doesn't do the event justice. I mean, let's start with the Brontës,' Hettie continued, getting into her stride. 'They turn up in that ridiculous camper van, assault Lavender Stamp – although for me that was a highlight – throw their weight around, reorganise the bookstall until they've created a riot, heckle the star turn, then chop his head off – and all that before they turn on each other. Add in a serious injury here and there, at least two death threats, a deadly asthma attack and an explosion to rival a low-budget Bond film, and what do we have?' Tilly held her breath, waiting for the punchline. 'We have a perfect snapshot of the publishing industry – competitive, greedy, unpleasant and spiteful.'

Tilly felt she should interrupt, if only for the sake of balance. 'Well, all those things certainly apply to Charlene Brontë, but I think you're being a bit harsh on the other two sisters. And Polly Hodge and Nicolette Upstart were nice.'

'That's not the point,' said Hettie. 'We could have had a couple of days by the sea in this heatwave, instead of chasing murderers across the memorial gardens at Furcross House.'

'But that *is* what we do,' said Tilly. 'We're the No. 2 Feline Detective Agency. We fix things when they go wrong.'

Tilly's words silenced Hettie. As always, her friend had given her a different perspective from the cross, bad-tempered world she inhabited, and – looking on the bright side, which Hettie rarely did – they had all survived to fight another day.

The knock on their door made both cats jump. Tilly answered, to find Betty Butter waving the *Sunday Snout* in the doorway. 'Seems you two are heroes again! Front page, then full story on pages three to eight. They've even dropped the gardening and style pages to make way for it all, although we've still got the crossword, thank goodness – Beryl would be beside herself if she couldn't sit down with her six across later. There's a few sausage rolls here for you to chew on while you read it.' Betty passed a plateful of hot pastries to Tilly along with the newspaper and returned to the bread ovens to rescue more treats for the afternoon survivors' tea.

Hettie pounced on the sausage rolls while Tilly filled the kettle. The two cats sat at the table, pawing over the weekend's drama through the eyes and words of Hacky Redtop, aided and abetted by pictorial backup from Prunella Snap and her Olympus Trip. Page after page unfolded the sorry tale of a literary festival derailed by Charlene Brontë's murderous deeds. The tableau took pride of place on the front page with the simple headline 'THE DEATH OF DOWNTON TABBY'; the inside pages carried pictures of Downton Tabby's arrival at the festival, the three Brontë sisters landing what seemed to be a collective punch on Lavender Stamp's nose, and a number of rather fine shots of Muddy Fryer in full flight during her Arthurian cycle.

'Oooh look! There you are, interviewing Downton Tabby on stage,' said Tilly, trying to contain her excitement. 'You look like one of those arty types who come on the telly late at night. And there's Polly and Nicolette eating a cream tea, and look – there's Betty and Beryl in the background. I think that's Delirium's paw you can see holding a cup and saucer. There's a lovely one of me with one of the Brontës. I'm not sure which one. It's a bit chilling to think it might have been Charlene. She seems to be smiling at my T-shirt.'

'Prunella Snap has excelled herself,' agreed Hettie, staring with interest at the coverage. 'It's hard to believe we were there at all except for these pictures. What a contrast – before and after the murders.'

'Yes, and before and after the stains on our T-shirts,' said Tilly, studying her picture a little closer.

'It's a shame they weren't around to capture the explosion at the end. The editorial's a bit out of date, but look, we've got a good mention on page three.' Hettie pulled the page towards her to read out loud. '"Once again, the town owes a great deed of gratitude to Hettie Bagshot and her intrepid staff at the No. 2 Feline Detective Agency, whose dogged determination and selfless bravery in such extreme and dangerous circumstances have won the day."'

Tilly clapped her paws with delight. 'See! That's just what I was saying earlier. It's what we do – fix things when they go wrong.'

Hettie conceded that Tilly was probably right, and posted another sausage roll into her mouth while her friend turned out the bottom drawer of the filing cabinet to look for a suitably clean T-shirt for the survivors' party.

CHAPTER TWENTY-ONE

On the understanding that they would help lay out the afternoon tea, Hettie and Tilly were invited upstairs to the Butters' kitchen to share in a 'bite to eat', as Beryl had put it. The reality was the biggest steak and kidney pie that Hettie had ever seen, accompanied by what Betty liked to call her Lancashire mash – a mountain of fluffy potatoes, drenched in butter and cream. The four cats tucked in with very little conversation, leaving enough pie and mash for a substantial extra portion which Hettie staggered down the garden to Bruiser's shed with.

The day was another hot one, and the garden was at ease with itself. The flowers which had bowed their heads against the torrential rain had turned their faces back up towards the sun, and the air was alive with bees, dancing from one flower to another. The scent from Beryl's roses was intoxicating; mixed with the aroma of steak and kidney pie, it gave Hettie the strange sensation of being in some far-off, perfect heaven.

Bruiser's stable door was open and he sat in a shaft of warm sunlight on an old armchair which he'd rescued from one of Lavender Stamp's refurbishments.

'The Butters have sent you some lunch,' Hettie said, positioning the plate close to his one good paw. She could see that the injuries brought about by Muddy Fryer's broadsword were still troubling him. Without asking, she broke the pie into small pieces and popped them into his mouth a bit at a time; the mash and gravy were delivered by spoon, but she left the final wiping of the plate to the patient, who managed to balance it on his good paw long enough to lick it clean.

'Catnip, that's what's needed here,' said Hettie, gathering up the empty plate and spoon. 'I'll be back in a minute.' She returned moments later with her catnip pouch and proceeded to fill Bruiser's pipe and then her own. Sitting with their backs to the shed, the two cats smoked their pipes in blissful peace, blowing smoke rings up into the cloudless sky. Bruiser's pain began to ease as the catnip took effect and Hettie dozed in the sun, letting the heightened murmurs of a perfect summer's day wash over her.

Their peace and quiet was shattered some time later as Lavender Stamp arrived to the clatter of deckchairs and trestle tables. Hettie opened one eye and took in the commotion which was now playing itself out on the lawn close to the house, and suddenly remembered that she was supposed to be helping with the tea party. The thought of engaging with the postmistress so soon after the festival debacle filled her with dread and, as Tilly approached, she looked across at Bruiser, envying him the bandages which constricted his movements.

'We could do with another pair of paws up there,' Tilly said, nodding in the direction of the chaos. 'Lavender's already caught her paw in a deckchair trying to put it up.'

'Pity it wasn't her neck,' grumbled Hettie, opening her other eye to get a clearer view. 'I'm not sure I can face seeing anyone this afternoon. I'm having one of my quiet moments.'

Tilly giggled. 'Well, I think you'll have to save that moment till later. Polly Hodge has just phoned to say she'll be making a significant announcement at the party and you wouldn't want to miss that, would you?'

'A significant announcement?' snorted Hettie, standing up. 'Whatever next? Perhaps she's found another bloody Brontë sister lurking on the Porkshire Moors!'

Tilly chose not to encourage another of Hettie's

261

soliloquies on the Brontës. Instead, she took her friend's arm and led her back up the garden path in time to see Lavender Stamp disappearing under a trestle table which had collapsed on top of her. Betty bustled out at the same moment, and – doing her best to control her laughter – suggested that the postmistress might like to 'cream and jam some scones' while Hettie and Tilly set up the seating and tables.

Lavender, grateful for the intervention, followed Betty inside, leaving Hettie and Tilly to their work. The two cats had just finished when they spied Poppa making his way up the path.

'Watcha! I've brought Miss Scarlet back from Furcross. I didn't think Bruiser would be up to driving her at the moment, so I've parked her in her shed.'

Tilly clapped her paws and hugged him. 'Thank you! I wondered how we could get her back. Now we're all home safe and sound.'

At that moment, Turner Page and Mr Pushkin arrived, sporting matching bow ties and waistcoats. They were swiftly followed by Jessie, adorned in what appeared to be a floaty red tent-frock, her ears circled with daisy chains. Hettie looked down at her own 'Born to be Mild' T-shirt and began to feel slightly underdressed until Meridian Hambone barged into the back yard on her disability scooter, wearing the last of her 'Littertray' merchandise; the shirt looked as if it had been run over several times before wrapping itself around the bony, ancient form of the town's hardware shop proprietor.

'Gawd love us!' she said, crashing into the trestle table that Hettie and Tilly had just finished putting up. 'These 'ere scooters never stops when you want 'em to. It's not like me biker days – I could stop on a sixpence in them days.'

Keen to cut off the flow of Meridian's transport history, Hettie disentangled the scooter from the table and pushed her across the lawn, leaving her in the company of Mr Pushkin. Tilly and Poppa rescued the table in time for Beryl to place a large samovar of tea on it. On cue, Delirium Treemints appeared, still wearing her pink skid lid, and took up her position to serve beverages as if she were connected to the tea urn by a magical gossamer thread.

Hilary and Cherry Fudge arrived next and made a beeline for the bottom of the garden, where they insisted on dressing Bruiser's injuries with clean bandages. Looking a little subdued, Bugs Anderton slid quietly into the garden and over to the tea urn, briefly severing the gossamer thread and giving Delirium a rare chance to mingle. Lavender Stamp and the Butter sisters made repeated journeys from kitchen to garden, filling the tables with delights. There were salmon sandwiches with the crusts cut off, sardine vol-au-vents, beef paste bridge rolls, mountains of crisps, cheese balls, miniature Cornish pasties, sausage rolls, cheese straws, dainty pork pies, cheese and bacon turnovers and a giant plate of small cooked sausages. The savoury table, as Beryl called it, was groaning under the sheer weight of the food and the party guests salivated in anticipation.

Closer to the back door, and taking up the only shade available in the garden, was the sweets and pudding table. By the time Lavender, Betty and Beryl had finished laying it out, the assembled company and those still arriving had to admit that it was a masterpiece of culinary magnificence. Tilly – delighted to see so many of her personal favourites gathered together on one table – decided to offer a running commentary, pointing to each individual item with her paw as she slowly made her way down the row.

'Cream and jam sponge, cream and chocolate sponge, cream and custard trifle, cream iced slices, custard tarts, chocolate eclairs with cream, coconut haystacks, pink and lemon iced fancies, butterfly buns, chocolate cornflake nests, and the biggest plateful of cream horns I've ever seen!' She had been playing to a captive audience, and, as she reached the end of the table, the guests clapped and stamped their feet, allowing Betty and Beryl to take a well-earned bow. Then the sisters passed out the paper plates, signalling that the tea party was well and truly underway.

As the cats came together to eat and share conversations in the sunshine, there was very little mention of the horror that had consumed them only a few hours before. It was as if there had been an unspoken decision to move on. There were, of course, a few matters still to be dealt with: the front of Furcross House would need a makeover to hide the inferno that had raged there; Bugs Anderton would need to come to terms with her brief romantic fling with Darius Bonnet; and Bruiser would, in the fullness of time, recover from his wounds.

Hettie watched as her friends moved around the garden, stopping to admire a flower here and there, at ease in each other's company and all sharing the badge of survival. She mused on what might have happened if Charlene Brontë had been allowed to continue her murderous rampage. Would she have killed again? If Poppa hadn't turned up when he did, Hettie was certain that she and Tilly would by now be lying somewhere on the Porkshire Moors with their throats cut. She shivered as the dark thoughts began to fill her mind. It had never occurred to her that running a detective agency could be such a perilous business. Perhaps they should quit while they were winning: a sweet shop on the high street would surely be a safer bet?

She was wrenched away from her considerations for the future by the arrival of Polly Hodge and Nicolette Upstart. The two crime writers were warmly welcomed and immediately issued with paper plates, which they filled and emptied in record time. Wiping the pastry from her whiskers with the back of her paw, Polly Hodge took centre stage on the Butters' lawn. The formidable white cat drew everyone's attention immediately, and all eating and conversation ceased as the cats gathered round, instinctively knowing that there was to be an announcement.

Satisfied that she had a captive audience, Polly addressed them. 'My friends – and after what we have all been through together, I think I may call you that – I must apologise for my late arrival at the party, but Nicolette and I have been engaged in negotiations of great excitement.' She paused for effect, leaving the crowd in no doubt that she was indeed the mistress of suspense, and Nicolette beamed one of her best smiles into the throng. 'The television company responsible for Downton Tabby's series, *In the Kitchen and Up the Stairs*, has asked me to produce a series of detective stories based on real cases to replace Sir Downton's programmes. I have asked Nicolette to assist me in this project, and there is only one final "i" to dot and "t" to cross.' Again the writer paused, but this time her steely gaze fell directly on Hettie. 'With the permission of Miss Hettie Bagshot,' she continued, 'I would like to call the new series *The No. 2 Feline Detective Agency*, starting with episode one, "The Death of Downton Tabby".'

Tilly dropped the cream horn she'd been quietly sucking and Hettie blushed red from her toes to the tips of her tabby ears. A cheer of approval went up as the cats raised and chinked their tea cups.

'Fame at last!' said Tilly, resisting the urge to dance a jig.

'And bang goes the sweet shop,' muttered Hettie, more to herself than anyone else.

ACKNOWLEDGEMENTS

I am indebted to Charlotte, Emily and Anne Brontë for inspiring me to write this book, and to the joy that Julian Fellowes has brought to the nation with his stories above and below stairs in Downton Abbey. I trust and believe that there is no greater compliment than a satirical swipe at the things we love and admire.

I would also like to thank Maddy Prior, Steeleye Span, Fairport Convention and Spriguns for making this book richer; and Nicolette Upstart for her continued love and support, in spite of everything!

Finally, to Polly Hodge, who – in life – held the prestigious position of P. D. James's cat. I'm sure they are both cooking up plots in some far and distant Elysian Field, remembered and greatly missed.

ACKNOWLEDGEMENTS